PRAISE FOR
KIM STANLEY ROBINSON'S
MARS BOOKS

RED MARS

"A high-water mark in novels of earth emigration . . . A tremendous achievement."
—*The Washington Post Book World*

"Absorbing . . . A scientifically informed imagination of rare ambition at work."
—*The New York Times Book Review*

"Staggering . . . The best novel on the colonization of Mars that has ever been written."
—Arthur C. Clarke

GREEN MARS

"The term 'epic' has been applied so often . . . that it has nearly lost any meaning beyond that of length. But Kim Stanley Robinson's latest, *Green Mars*, earns the appellation as few works ever have. . . . Dense as a diamond and as sharp; it makes even most good novels seem pale and insignificant by comparison."
—*The Washington Post Book World*

"Grand in scope, meticulous in detail."
—*The New York Times Book Review*

"One of the major sagas of the [latest] generation in science fiction."
—*Chicago Sun-Times*

Books by Kim Stanley Robinson

FICTION

The Mars Trilogy
Red Mars
Green Mars
Blue Mars (forthcoming)

The California Trilogy
The Wild Shore
The Gold Coast
Pacific Edge

Escape from Kathmandu
A Short, Sharp Shock
Green Mars (novella)
The Blind Geometer
The Memory of Whiteness
Icehenge
The Planet on the Table
Remaking History

NONFICTION

The Novels of Philip K. Dick

BANTAM BOOKS

New York
Toronto
London
Sydney
Auckland

KIM STANLEY ROBINSON

A SHORT,
SHARP
SHOCK

This edition contains the complete text
of the original hardcover edition
NOT ONE WORD HAS BEEN OMITTED.
A SHORT, SHARP SHOCK

A Bantam Spectra Book / published by arrangement
with the author

PUBLISHING HISTORY
Mark V. Ziesing edition published 1990
Bantam edition / March 1996

SPECTRA and the portrayal of a boxed "s" are trademarks
of Bantam Books, a division of Bantam Doubleday Dell Publishing Group, Inc.

ISBN 0-553-57461-2

Published simultaneously in the United States and Canada

Bantam Books are published by Bantam Books, a division of Bantam
Doubleday Dell Publishing Group, Inc. Its trademark, consisting of the
words "Bantam Books" and the portrayal of a rooster, is Registered in
U.S. Patent and Trademark Office and in other countries. Marca Reg-
istrada. Bantam Books, 1540 Broadway, New York, New York 10036.

PRINTED IN THE UNITED STATES OF AMERICA

RAD   0 9 8 7 6 5 4 3 2 1

A SHORT, SHARP SHOCK

ONE

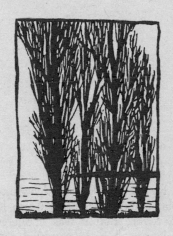

THE
NIGHT
BEACH

When he came to he was drowning. The water was black and he bobbed up in it swiftly, obscurely aware that it was dangerous to do so, but he was helpless to stop; he tumbled over and swam downward, arms loose and thrusting like tentacles, but it was useless. Air popped out of him in a stream of white bubbles that flattened and shimmied as they squashed upward, all clustered around bearing him to the surface. He glanced up, suddenly aware of the idea of surface; and there it was, an undulating sheet of obsidian silk on which chips of raw silver skittered wildly back and forth. A flock of startled birds turning all at once — no — it was, he thought as the world began to roar, the shattered image of a crescent moon. At the thought a whole cosmology bloomed in him —

And broke apart like the moon's image, as he crashed up into the air and gasped. He flailed at the water whooping and kicking hard to stay afloat; he felt a wave lift him, and flopped around to face it. A cold smack in the face and he tumbled again, thrashed through a somersault and came up breathing, barking like a seal to suck in more air.

The next time under he rammed a sandbar and then he was rolling on a steep shorebreak, sluiced by sandy water and struck repeatedly by small silver fish. He crawled up through rushing foam, mouth full of salty grit, hands sinking wrist-deep in the wet sand. The little fish leaped in the phosphorescent foam, banged into his arms and legs. The beach was bouncing with silver fish, it was like an infestation of insects. On hands and knees he couldn't avoid squashing some into the sand.

At the high water mark he collapsed. He looked across a gleaming black strand, filigreed with sea foam receding on a wave. Coarse-grained sand sparked with reflected moonlight, and the fish arched to the shape of the crescent moon, which hung over the horizon at the end of a mirrorflake path of water. Such a dense, intricate, shifting texture of black and white—

A large wave caught him, rolled him back down among the suffocating fish. He clawed the sand without effect, then slammed into another body, warm and as naked as he was. The receding wave rushed down to the triple ripple of the low water mark, leaving them behind: he and a woman, a woman with close-cropped hair. She appeared senseless and he tried to pull her up, but the next wave knocked them down and rolled them like driftwood. He untangled himself from her and got to his knees, took her arms and pulled her up the wet sand, shifting one knee at a time, the little silver fish bouncing all around them. When he had gotten her a few body lengths into dry sand he fell beside her. He couldn't move.

From down the beach came shrill birdy cries. Children ran up to them shouting, buckets swinging at the ends of their arms like great deformed hands.

When they ran on he could not move his head to track them. They returned to his field of vision, with taller people whose heads scraped the moon. The children dashed up and down the strand on the lace edge of the waves. They dumped full buckets of wriggling silver leaves in a pile beyond his head. Fire bloomed and driftwood was thrown on it, until transparent gold ribbons leaped up into the night.

Then another wave caught them and rolled them back down to the sea; the tide was rising and they would have perished, but the cords of a thrown net stopped them short, and they were hauled back and dumped closer to the fire, which hissed and sizzled. The children were laughing.

Later, fighting unconsciousness, he lifted the great stone at the end of his neck. The fire had died, the moon sat on the beach. He looked at the woman beside him. She lay on her stomach, one knee to the side. Dry sand stuck to her skin and the moonlight reflecting from her was gritty; it sparkled as she breathed. Powerful thighs met in a rounded muscly bottom, which curved the light into the dip of her lower back. Her upper back was broad, her spine in a deep trough of muscle, her shoulders rangy, her biceps thick. Short-cropped hair, dark under the moon's glaze, curled tight to her head; and the profile glimpsed over one shoulder was straight-nosed and somehow classical: a swimmer, he thought as his head fell back, with the big chest and smooth hard muscling of a sponge diver, or a sea goddess, something from the myths of a world he couldn't remember.

Then her arm shifted out, and her hand came to rest against his flank, and the feel of her coursed all through him: a short, sharp shock. He caught his breath and found he was sitting up facing her, her palm both cool and warm against his side. He watched her catch the moon on her skin and fling it away.

TWO

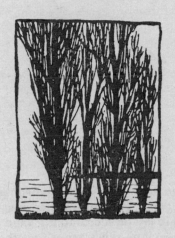

SEA
WRACK

When he woke in the morning, the woman was gone. The sun burned just over the water. He lay on a crumbling sand cliff, the high mark of the previous tide's assault on the beach. With his head resting on one ear, he saw a wet slick foam-flecked strand of silvery brown, and the sea; resting on the other, he saw a lumpy expanse of blond beach, dotted with driftwood. Behind the beach was a forest, which rose steeply to a very tall cliff of white stone; its top edge made a brilliant border with the deep blue sky above.

He lifted his head and noticed that the sand cliff under him was a tiny model of the granite cliff standing over the forest—a transient replica, already falling into the sea. But then again the immense rock cliff was also falling into the sea, the forest its beach, the beach its strand. It repeated the little sand cliff's dissolution on a scale of time so much vaster that the idea of it made him dizzy. The tide ebbs and the stars die.

On the wet strand a troop of birds ran back and forth. They seemed a kind of sandpiper, except their feathers were a dark metallic red. They stabbed away at dead grunion rolling in the wrack, and then dashed madly up the strand chased by waves, their stick legs pumping over blurred reflections of themselves. They made one of these frantic cavalry charges right under a thick white fishing line; surprised at the sight, he raised himself up on his elbows and looked behind him.

A surf fisher sat on a big driftwood log. In fact there were several of them, scattered down the beach at more or less regular intervals. The one closest to him was all in brown, an old brown woman in a baggy coat and floppy hat, who waved briefly at him and did not stir from her log.

He stood and walked to her. Beside her a bucket stood on the sand, filled with the little silver fish from the previous night. She gestured at the bucket, offering him some of the fish, and he saw that her hand was a thick mass of shiny dark brown, her fingers long tubes of lighter hollow brown, with bulbs at their ends. Like tubes of seaweed. And her coat was a brown frond of kelp, and her face a wrinkled brown bulb, popped by the slit of her mouth; and her eyes were polyps, smooth and wet

An animated bundle of seaweed. He knew this was wrong, but there she sat, and the sun was bright and it was hard to think. Many things inside his head had broken or gone away. He felt no particular emotion. He sat on the sand beside her fishing pole, trying to think. There was a thick tendril that fell from her lower back to her driftwood log, attaching her to it.

He found he was puzzled. "Were you here last night?" he croaked.

The old woman cackled. "A wild one. The stars fell and the fish tried to become birds again. Spring."

She had a wet hissing voice, a strange accent. But it was his language, or a language he knew. He couldn't decide if he knew any others or not.

She gestured again at her bucket, repeating her offer. Noticing suddenly the pangs of his hunger, he took a few grunion from the bucket and swallowed them.

When he had finished he said, "Where is the woman who washed up with me?"

She jerked a thumb at the forest behind them. "Sold to the spine kings."

"Sold?"

"They took her, but they gave us some hooks."

He looked up at the stone cliff above the trees, and she nodded.

"Up there, yes. But they'll take her on to Kataptron Cove."

"Why not me?"

"They didn't want you."

A child ran down the beach toward them, stepping on the edge of the sand cliff and collapsing it with her passage. She too wore a baggy frond coat and a floppy hat. He noticed that each of the seated surf fishers had a child running about in its area. Buckets sat on the sand like discarded party hats. For a long time he sat and watched the child approach. It was hard to think. The sunlight hurt his eyes.

"Who am I?" he said.

"You can't expect me to tell you that," the fisher-woman said.

"No." He shook his head. "But I . . . I don't know who I am."

"We say, the fish knows it's a fish when we yank it into the air."

He got to his feet, laughed oddly, waited for the blood to return to his head. "Perhaps I'm a fish, then.

But ... I don't know what's happened to me. I don't know what happened."

"Whatever happened, you're here." She shrugged and began to reel in her line. "It's now that matters, we say."

He considered it.

"Which way is the cove you mentioned?" he said at last.

She pointed down the beach, away from the sun. "But the beach ends, and the cliff falls straight into the sea. It's best to climb it here."

He looked at the cliff. It would be a hard climb. He took a few more grunion from the bucket. Fellow fish, dead of self-discovery. The seaweed woman grubbed in a dark mass of stuff in the lee of her log, then offered him a skirt of woven seaweed. He tied it around his waist, thanked her and took off across the beach.

"You'd better hurry," she called after him. "Kataptron Cove is a long way west, and the spine kings are fast."

THREE

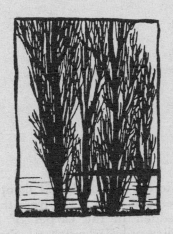

THE SPINE

The forest was thick and damp, with leaves scattered at every level, from the rotting logs embedded in the carpet of ferns to the sunbroken ceiling of leaves overhead. Streams gurgled down the slope, but apparently it had not rained for some time, as smaller creekbeds held only trickles; one served him as a pebble-bottomed trail, broken by networks of exposed roots. In the cool gloom he hiked uphill, moving from glade to glade as if from one green room to the next, each sculpted according to a different theory of space and color. Leaves everywhere gave proof of his eye's infinite depth of field, and all was still except for the water falling to the sea—and an occasional flash in his peripheral vision, birds, perhaps, which he could never quite see.

The forest ended at the bottom of the cliff, which rose overhead like the side of an enormous continent. Boulders taller than the trees were scattered about at the foot of the cliff. Ferns and mosses covered the

tumble of rotten granite between boulders. The cliff itself was riven by deep gullies, which were almost as
steep as the buttresses separating them. He clambered
between boulders looking for a likely way up, in a
constant fine mist: far above waterfalls had broken
apart, and to the left against the white rock was a
broad faint rainbow.

Just as he was concluding that he would have to
scramble up one of the gulleys he came on a trail going up the side of one, beginning abruptly in the ferny
talus. The trail was wide enough for two people to
walk side by side, and had been hacked out of the
granite wall of the gully, where it switchbacked frequently. When the side wall became completely vertical, the trail wound out over the buttress to the left
and zigzagged up that steep finger of stone, in stub-
born defiance of the breathtaking exposure. It was impossible to imagine how the trail had been built, and
it was also true that a break anywhere in the supporting walls would have cut the trail as neatly as
miles of empty air; but there were no breaks, and the
weedless gravel and polished bedrock he walked over
indicated frequent use. He climbed as if on a staircase
in a dream, endlessly ascending in hairpin turns, until
the forest and beach below became no more than
green and blond stripes running as far as he could see
in both directions, between the sunbeaten blue of the
ocean and the sunbeaten white of the granite.

Then the cliff laid back, and the trail led straight
ahead on an incline that got less and less steep, until
he saw ahead a skyline of shattered granite, running
right to left as far as he could see. The rock stood
stark against the sky. He hurried forward and suddenly he was on the crest of a ridge extending to his
left and right, and before him he saw ocean again —
ocean far below, spread out in front of him exactly as
it was behind. Surprised, he walked automatically to a

point where he could see all the way down: a steep cliff, a strip of forest, a strip of sand, the white-on-blue tapestry of breaking waves, the intense cobalt of the sea. He stepped back and staggered a little, trying to look in every direction at once.

He was standing on the crest of a tall peninsula, which snaked through an empty ocean for as far as he could see. It was a narrow ridge of white granite, running roughly east to west, bisecting the blue plate of the sea and twice marring the circular line of the horizon. The ridge rose to peaks again and again, higher perhaps in the talcum of afternoon light to the west; it also undulated back and forth, big S shapes making a frozen sine wave. The horizon was an enormous distance away, so far away that it seemed wrong to him, as wrong as the seaweed woman. In fact the whole prospect was fantastically strange; but there he stood, feeling the wind rake hard over the lichen-stained ridge, watching it shove at low shrubs and tufts of sedge.

It occurred to him that the peninsula extended all the way around the world. A big ocean world, and this lofty ring of rock its only land: he was sure of it. It was as if it were something he remembered.

FOUR

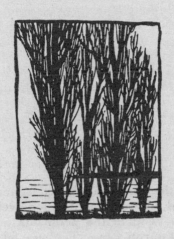

BEAUTY IS
THE PROMISE OF
HAPPINESS

And the only happiness is action. So he roused himself and headed west, thinking that a bend in the peninsula out that way might hide Kataptron Cove. The sun fell just to the right of the rock, slowing as it fell, flattening as if reluctant to touch the horizon, breaking into bands of glowing orange light that stretched until they were sucked down by the sea. The twilight was long, a mauve and purple half day, and he hiked rapidly over the crest's shattered granite, which was studded with crystals of translucent quartz. As he walked over the rough edges of stones, feeling liberty in the twisting ligaments of his ankles, he kept an eye out for some sort of shelter for the night. The trail he had followed onto the spine had disappeared, no doubt because the crest itself served as a broad high trail; but at one point a deep transverse cleft had been filled at a single spot by boulders, confirming his notion that the trail still ran, and would reappear when needed.

So he was not surprised when he came upon a low circular stone hut, next to a small pool of water. In this area stone broke away from the bedrock in irregular plates, and a great number of these had been gathered and stacked in rings that grew successively smaller as they got higher off the ground, until a final large capstone topped things off. The stones had been sized and placed so precisely that it would have been difficult to get more than a fingernail between any two of them. A short chimney made of smaller stones protruded from one side of the roof.

Opening a wooden door in the wall opposite the chimney, he entered and found a wooden shelf circling the interior of the wall. Next to the fireplace was a stack of kindling and logs; other than that the hut was empty. He was without the means to start a fire, and it was fairly warm in any case, so he went back outside and drank from the pool, then sat against the west wall to eat the last of the fisher-woman's grunion, in the final hour of twilight. As the light leaked out of the sky it turned a deep rich blue, dark but not quite black: and across this strangely palpable firmament the stars popped into existence, thousands upon thousands of them, from bright disks that might have been nearby planets to dots so faint that he could only see them by looking slightly to the side. Eventually the sky was packed with stars, so densely that they defined perfectly the dome of sky; and frightened him. "Where I come from there are not so many stars," he said shakily to the hut, and then felt acutely his solitude, and the emptinesses inside his mind, the black membranes he could not penetrate. He retreated into the hut. After a long time lying on the hard wooden shelf, he fell asleep.

Sometime before dawn he was awakened by a crowd of folk banging in the doorway. They held him down and searched under his skirt. They had broad

hard hands. Cloaks made of small leaves sewn together clicked in the dark, and it smelled like oranges.

"Are you the spine kings?" he asked, drunk with
sleep.

They laughed, an airy sound. One said, "If we
were you'd be strangled with your own guts by now."

"Or tossed down the cliff."

The first voice said, "Or both. The spine kings'
hello."

They all had lumps on their left shoulders, irregular dark masses that looked like shrubs. They took
him out of the hut, and under the sea-colored sky he
saw that the lumps were in fact shrubs—miniature
fruit trees, it appeared, growing out of their left shoulders. The fruits were fragrant and still reminded him
of oranges, although the smell had been altered by the
salt tang, made more bitter. Round fruit, in any case,
of a washed-out color that in better light might have
been pale green.

The members of this group arranged themselves in
a circle facing inward, took off their leaf cloaks and sat
down. He sat in the circle between two of them, glanc-
ing at the shoulder tree to his right. It definitely grew
directly out of the creature's skin—the gnarled little
roots dove into the flesh just as a wart would, leaving
an overgrown fissure between bark and skin.

With a jerk he looked away. It was almost dawn,
and the treefolk began singing a low monophonic
chant, in a language he didn't recognize. The sky light-
ened to its day blue, slightly thickened by the sun's absence, and the wind suddenly picked up, as if a door
had banged open somewhere—a cool fresh breeze,
peeling over the spine in the same moment that the
sun pricked the distant gray line of the horizon, a
green point stretching to a line of hot yellow and then
a band of white fire, throwing the sea's surface into
shadow and revealing a scree of low diaphanous

cloud. Before the sun had detached itself from the sea each member of the circle had plucked a fruit from the shoulder of the person on their right, and when the sun was clear and the horizon sinking rapidly away from it, they ate. Their bites caused a faint crystalline ringing, and the odor of bitter oranges was strong. He felt his stomach muscles contract, and saliva ran down his throat. The celebrant nearest the sun glanced at him and said, "Treeless here will be hungry."

He almost nodded, but held himself still.

"What's your name?" the celebrant asked. He had been the first speaker in the hut.

"I don't know."

"No?" The creature considered it. "Treeless will be good enough, then. In our naming language, that is *Thel*."

In his mind he called himself Thel. But his real name . . . black space, behind his nose, in the sky under his skull. . . . "It will do here," he said, and waved a hand. "It is accurate enough."

The man laughed. "So it is. I am Julo." He looked across the circle. "Garth, come here."

A young man stood. He had been sitting opposite Julo, facing out from the circle, and now Thel noticed his tree grew from the right shoulder rather than the left.

"This is Garth, which means Rightbush. Garth, give Thel here an apple." Garth hesitated, and Julo strode across the circle of watchers and cuffed him on the arm. "Do it!"

Garth approached Thel and stood before him, looked down. Thel said to him, "Which should I choose?"

With a grateful glance up the youth indicated the largest fruit, on a lower branch. Thel took the round green sphere in his fingers and pulled sharply, noting Garth's involuntary wince. Then he sniffed the stem, and bit through the skin. The bitter taste of orange, he sat in a small dark room, watching the wick of a lamp lit by a match held in long fingers, the flame turned up and burning poorly, in a library with bookcases for walls and a huge old leather globe in one corner. . . . He shook his head, back on the windy dawn spine, Julo's laughter in his ear, behind that a crystalline ringing. A bird hovered in the updraft, a windhover searching the lee cliff for prey. "Thank you," Thel said to Garth.

The treefolk gathered around him, touched his bare shoulders, asked him questions. He had nothing but questions in reply. Who were the spine kings? he asked, and their faces darkened. "Why do you ask?" Julo said. "Why don't you know?"

Thel explained. "The fisherfolk pulled me from the sea. Before that—I don't know. I can't . . ." He shook his head. "They pulled out a woman with me, a swimmer, and sold her to the spine kings." He gestured helplessly, the thought of her painful. Already the memory of her was fading, he knew. But that touch in the moonlight—"I want to find her."

"They have some of our people as well," Julo said. "We're going after them." He reached into his bag and threw Thel a leaf cloak and a pair of leather moccasins with thick soles. "You can come along. They're at Kataptron Cove, for the sacrifices."

The boy's fruit was suddenly heavy on his stomach, and he shuddered as if every cell in him had tasted something bitter.

FIVE

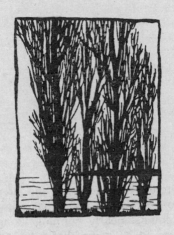

THE SNAKE
AND THE TREE

The treefolk hiked long and hard, following a line on the broad crest that minimized the ups and downs, nearly running along a rock road that Thel judged to be some three thousand feet above the sea. After a few days, the south side of the sinuous peninsula became a fairly gentle slope, cut by ravines and covered with tall redwood trees; in places on this side the beach was a wide expanse, dotted with ponds and green with rippling dune grass. The north side, on the other hand, remained a nearly vertical cliff, falling directly into waves, which slapped against the rock unbroken and sent bowed counterwaves back out to the north, stippling the blue surface of the water with intersecting arcs.

Once their ridge road narrowed, and big blocky towers of pink granite stood in their way. The trail reappeared then, on the sunny southern slope, and they followed it along a contoured traverse below the boulders, passing small pools that looked hacked into the rock. Half a day of this and they had passed the sharp peaks and were back on the ridge, looking ahead down its back as it snaked through the blue ocean. "How long is this peninsula?" Thel asked, but they only stared at him.

Every morning at sunrise Julo ordered young Garth to provide a shoulder apple for Thel's consumption, and in the absence of any other food Thel accepted it and ate hungrily. He saw no more hallucinations, but each time experienced a sudden flush of pinkness in his vision, and felt the bitter tang of the taste to his bones. His right shoulder began to ache as he lay down to sleep. He ignored it and hiked on. He noticed that on cloudy days his companions hiked more slowly, and that when they stopped by pools to rest on those days, they took off their boots and stuck their feet between cracks in the rock, looking weary and relaxed.

Some days later the peninsula took a broad curve to the north, and for the first time the sun set on the south side of it. They stopped at a hut set on a particularly high knob on the ridge, and Thel looked around at the peninsula, splitting the ocean all the way to the distant horizon. It was a big world, no doubt of it; and the days and nights were much longer than what he had been used to, he was sure. He grew tired at midday, and often woke for a time in the middle of the long nights. "It doesn't make sense," he said to Garth, waving perplexed at the mountainous mound zigzagging across the sea. "There isn't any geological process that could create a feature like this."

This was said almost in jest, given the other more important mysteries of his existence. But Garth stared at him, eyes feverish. He was lying exhausted, his feet deep in a crack; seeing this in the evenings Thel always resolved not to eat, and every morning he awoke too ravenous to refuse. Now, as if to pay Garth back with conversation, he added, "Land floats like wood, thick cakes of it drifting on slow currents of melted rock below, and a peninsula like this, as tall as this . . . I suppose it could be a mid-oceanic ridge, but in that case it would be volcanic, and this is all granite. I don't understand."

Garth said, "It's here, so it must be possible."

Thel laughed. "The basis of your world's philosophy. You didn't tell me you were a philosopher."

Garth smiled bitterly. "Live like me and you too will become one. Maybe it's happening already, eh? Maybe before you swam ashore you didn't concern yourself with questions like that."

"No," Thel said, considering it. "I was always curious. I think." And to Garth's laugh: "So it feels, you see. Perhaps not everything is gone." It seemed possible that the questions came from the shattered side of his mind, from some past self he couldn't recall but which shaped his thinking anyway. "Perhaps I studied rock."

At sunset the wind tended to die, just as the sunrise quickened it; now it slackened. Perhaps I have died like the wind, he thought; perhaps the only thing that survives after death are the questions, or the habit of questioning.

The two of them watched the sun sink, just to the left of the bump of the spine on the horizon. "It's as if it's a river in reverse," Thel said. "If a deep river ran across a desert land, and then you reversed the landscape, water and earth, you would get something that looked like this."

"The earth river," Garth said. "The priests of the birdfolk call it that."

"Are there any tributaries? Any lakes-turned-into-islands?"

"I've never seen any."

The air darkened and the salt air grew chill. Garth was breathing deeply, about to fall asleep, when he said in a voice not his, a voice pleasant but at the same time chilling: "Through mirrors we see things right way round at last."

* * *

In the days that followed, this image of a landscape in reverse haunted Thel, though in the end it explained nothing. The stony spine continued to split the water, and it got taller, the south side becoming as steep as the north again. In places they walked on a strip of level granite no wider than a person, and on each side the cliffs plunged some five thousand feet into white foam tapestries that shifted back and forth over deep water, as if something below the blue were lightly breathing: it disturbed one's balance to look down at it, and though the strip was wide enough to walk on comfortably, the sheer airiness of it gave Thel vertigo. Garth walked over it with a pinched expression, and Julo laughed at him, cuffed him hard so that he had to go to his knees to avoid falling over the side; then Julo forced him to walk backwards, which served the others as amusement.

Eventually the north side grew less steep, laying out until the peninsula was wider than ever. In this section a hot white cliff faced south, a cool forested slope faced north. On the north slope were scattered stands of enormous evergreens, the tallest trees three or four hundred feet high. One of these giants stood on a ledge just below the crest, and had grown up above the ridge, where the winds had flattened it so that its branches grew horizontally in all directions, some laying over the ridge, others fanning out into the air over the beach and the sea far below.

The treefolk greeted this flat-topped giant as an ancestor, and clambered out over the horizontal branches to the tree's mighty trunk, over it, and out the other side. They ended up on three or four lightning-blasted gnarly branches, ten feet wide and so solid that jumping up and down would not move them, though the whole tree swayed gently in a fitful west wind. Big shallow circular depressions had been cut into the tops of these branches, and the exposed wood had been polished till it gleamed.

They spent the night in these open-roofed rooms, under the star-flooded sky. By starlight Thel looked at the wood by his head and saw the grain of centuries of growth exposed. The peninsula had been here for thousands of years, millions of years—both the plant life and the erosion of the granite showed that. But how had it begun? "When you talk among yourselves about the spine," he said to the treefolk, "do you ever talk about where it came from? Do you have a story that explains it?"

Julo was looking down into the grain of the floor beneath him, still and rapt as if he had not heard Thel; but after a while he said, in a low voice, "We tell a story about it. Traveling in silent majesty along their ordered ways, the gods tree and snake were lovers in the time without time. But they fell into time, and snake saw a vision of a lover as mobile as he, and he chased round the sky until he saw the vision was his own tail. He bit the tail in anger and began to bleed, and his blood flowed out into a single great drop, bound by the circle his long body made. He died of the loss, and tree climbed on his back and drove her roots deep into his body, trying to feed his blood into him, trying to bring him back to life, and all her acorns dropped and grew to join in the attempt. And here we are, accidents of her effort, trying to help her as we can, and some day the snake will live again, and we will all sail off among the stars, traveling in silent majesty."

"Ah," Thel said. And then: "I see."

But he didn't see, and he arranged himself for sleep and looked up into the thickets of stars, disappointed. Garth lay next to him, and much later, when the others were asleep, he whispered to him, "You don't know where you came from. You have no idea how you came here or what you are. Worry about that, and when you know those things, then worry about the great spine."

SIX

KATAPTRON
COVE

The next dawn it was bitterly cold out on the swaying branches, and they sat back against the curved wall of the biggest room shivering as Julo watched the sky to determine the exact moment of sunrise, hidden behind the ridge. When he turned to pluck the fruit from the man next to him he took three, and the others did the same. Thel restricted himself to his usual one of Garth's, and asked him why the others had eaten more.

"We'll reach Kataptron Cove this evening."

And so they did. It was on the south side, in an arc the peninsula made. Here the granite side of the peninsula was marred by the shattered walls of a small crater—a horseshoe ring of jagged black rock, extending into the sea and broken open to it at its outermost point, so that the inside of the crater was a small lagoon. Clearly it was an old volcanic vent, and as it was the first sign of vulcanism that Thel had seen, he approached it with interest.

But he was soon distracted by the grim faces of the treefolk, who marched around him as if going into battle. Foreboding charged the air, and the treefolk abandoned the trail that descended the southern slope in a long traverse to the crater bay, and struggled through dense woods above the trail.

They descended into thick salt air filled with the sound of waves, gliding from tree to tree like spirits, moving very slowly onto the high crumbly rim of the crater overlooking the inner lagoon; the curving inner wall of the crater was a reddish cliff, overgrown with green. Where the crater met the spine a stream fell down the inner wall and across the sand into the lagoon; on the banks of the stream there was a permanent camp, built in a grove of trees that had been cleared of undergrowth. In the shadows of these trees people moved, and smoke spiraled up through the sunbeams lancing among the branches.

In the depths of the grove there was a hubbub, and a crowd emerged onto the open beach, a gang wearing leather skirts and belted short swords, and tight golden helmets. They chivvied along a short row of prisoners, naked and in chains, and Thel heard Garth whimper softly. He looked around and saw that the treefolk had their eyes fixed on the beach in horror, and unwilling fascination. "What is it?" he said.

Garth pointed at where the grove met the beach. Two tall tree trunks standing beside each other had been stripped bare; behind the trunks stood a platform about half their height. "It's the flex X," Garth whispered, and would not elaborate. He sat with his back to the scene, head in hands.

Thel and the rest of the treefolk watched as a prisoner was hauled up the steps of the platform. Two crews on the ground set about winding ropes tied to the top of each tree trunk, until the trunks were crossing each other at about the level of the platform. Intuitively Thel understood the function of the large bowed X the trees made, and his stomach contracted to a hard knot of tension and vicarious terror; still he watched as the first prisoner was tied to the two trees, and the thick ropes holding the trees in position were knocked off notched stumps, and the two tall trunks returned to an upright position, with a stately swaying motion that had not the slightest hitch in it when the prisoner was ripped apart. Blood fountained from the head and the body, now separated. Thel saw that the beach around the two trees was littered with lumps here and there, all a dark brown, now splattered with red: the wreckage of lives.

At that distance people were the size of dolls, and they heard nothing of them over the sounds of waves. The executioners tied each prisoner to the two trees in a different manner, so that the second came apart at the limbs, and the third in the middle, leaving a long loop of intestine hanging between the two poles.

Thel found he was sitting. His skin was covered with a sour sweat. He felt cold. He moved in front of Garth, took his face in his hands. "The spine kings?"

Garth nodded miserably.

"Who are they?"

No response. Feeling the futility of the question, Thel stood and went to Julo, who laughed maliciously as he saw Thel's face.

"What will you do?" Thel asked.

"Go have a look. They'll be drinking tonight, they'll all get drunk and there'll be little watch kept. They fear no one in any case. We can be quiet, and some of us will go have a look for our kind. If we can find them, we can see what kind of lock they're under. It may be possible to slip them out on a night like this. We're lucky to have seen that," he said, ironic to the point of snarling. "We know they'll be off guard."

Thel nodded, impressed despite himself by Julo's

courage. "I want to come with you," he said. "I can look for the swimmer."

"She'll be under stronger guard," Julo warned him. "But you're welcome to try. It's why you're here, right?"

SEVEN

TWO XS

So in the long indigo twilight they made their way around the rim of the crater bay like ghosts, stepping so silently that the loudest sound coming from them was their heartbeats, tocking at the backs of their open mouths. Shadows with heartbeats, as silent as the fear of death, slipping from trunk to trunk and searching the forest ahead with the acute gaze of hunted beasts ... the spine king sentinels carried crossbows, Julo had said. They descended the crater wall well away from the village, and then worked their way back to it through a thin forest of pines, stepping across a carpet of brown needles.

Ahead came the sound of voices, and the beach stream. The leaves of the treefolk's shoulder bushes rustled when they moved too quickly. It was getting dark, the color draining out of everything except the pinpricks of fire dancing in the black needles ahead.

Drumming began, parodying their heavy heartbeats. They hugged the crater wall, circled to the edge of a firelit clearing. In the clearing were huts, cages, and platforms, all made of straight branches with the bark still on them. Some of the cages held huddled figures.

Thel froze. Reflection of torchlight from a pair of eyes, the shaggy head of a wild beast captured and caged, brilliant whites defiant and exhausted: it was her. Thel stared and stared at the black lump of the body, heavy in the dark, clothed only in dirt—the tangled hair backlit by fire—eyes reflecting torchlight. He had no idea why he was so certain. But he knew it was the swimmer.

The treefolk were clustered around him. When guards with torches arrived in the clearing, the prisoners sat up, and around him Thel heard a faint rustling of leaves. He peered more closely and saw that the cage beside the swimmer's held seated figures, slumped over. One of them begged for water and the guards approached. In the sharply flickering torchlight Thel could see slack faces, eyes shut against the light, odd hunched shoulders—ah. Trunks, stalks, stumps: their shoulder bushes had been chopped off. One of the captured treefolk, lying flat on the ground, was hauled up; he still had his little tree, its fruit gone, its leaves drooping. "The fire's low," one guard said drunkenly, and drew his short broadsword and hacked away. It took several blows, *thunk, thunk*, the victim weeping, his companions listless, looking away, the other guards holding the victim upright and steady and finally bending the trunk of the miniature tree until it broke with a dull crack. The victim flopped to the ground and the guards left the cage and tossed the little tree onto the embers of a big fire: it flared up white and burned well for several minutes, as if the wood were resinous.

Thel's companions had watched this scene without moving; only the rustle of leaves betrayed their distress. The guards left and they slipped back into the black forest, and Thel followed them. When they showed no signs of stopping he crashed forward recklessly, and pulled at Julo's arm; when Julo shrugged him off and continued on, Thel reached out and grabbed the trunk of Julo's shoulder tree and yanked him around, and then had to defend himself immediately from a vicious rain of blows, which stopped only when the other treefolk threw themselves between the two, protesting in anxious mutters, whispering *shh, shh, shhh.*

"What are you doing?" Thel cried softly.

"Leaving," Julo said between his teeth.

"Aren't you going to free them?"

"They're dead." Julo turned away, clearly too disgusted and furious to discuss it further. With a fierce chopping gesture he led the others away.

"What about the swimmer?"

They didn't stop. Suddenly the black forest seemed filled with distant voices, with drunken bodies crashing into underbrush, with yellow winking torches bouncing through the trees. Thel backed into a tree, leaned against the shaggy bark. He took deep deliberate breaths. The cage had been made of lashed branches, but out in the center of the clearing like that. . . .

"I'll help you," Garth said out of the darkness, giving Thel a start. "It's me, Garth."

They held each other's forearms in the dark. "You'll lose the others if you stay," Thel said.

"I know," Garth said, voice low and bitter. "You've seen how he treats me. I want to be free of them all, forever. I'll make my own life from now on."

"That's not an easy thing," Thel said.

Without replying Garth turned back the way they had come, and they crept back to the clearing. Once there they lay behind a fallen log and looked

into the firelit cages. Garth's fellow folk sat there list-
lessly.

"Their trees won't grow back?"

"Would your arm?"

"And so they'll die?"

"Yes."

Garth slipped away, and after a time Thel saw an
orange light like a sort of firefly bobbing through the
trees: Garth, holding a branch tipped by a glowing
ember. Thel joined him, and they crept to the back of
the treefolk's cage, and Garth held the tip of the
branch to the lashings at the bottom of one pole. As
they blew on the coal the treefolk inside watched,
without a sound or any sign of interest.

Garth begged those inside to emerge, and got no
reply. Thel stared at the orange ember which bright-
ened as they blew on it, embarrassed for Garth, and
worried about what he could do alone. When the cage
lashing caught fire with a miniature explosion of white
flame, Garth looked at his comrades through the
smoke and said fiercely, "You know what the spine
kings have done to you! You know what they'll do to
you next! Come out and exact some revenge, meet
your end like trees should. While you do we can rescue a friend who yet lives, and you'll either make a
quick end to it, or escape to be free on the great spine
when your time comes." He jerked hard on the pole
and it came loose. "Come on, get out there among
them and remember the part of you they threw
on their fires."

One of them started forward and crawled under
the lifted pole, and the rest looked at each other, at the
raw stumps protruding from their shoulders; they too
slipped from the cage. In a moment they had all disappeared into the dark.

"It would be better if we had something else for

the other cage," Garth said to Thel. "The ember is dying."

"There are a lot more in the fire."

"My kin's lives."

"They can free these others."

Garth nodded. "We burn hot. But one of those swords they carry would be helpful." And he disappeared again.

Thel waited, as near the swimmer's cage as he could get without emerging into the light. From the hut beside the bonfire and the central cage came the sounds of laughter, then those of an argument turning ugly. Around him in the forest were odd noises, sudden silences, and he imagined the treeless treefolk wandering murderously in the dark, jumping drunken guards as they stumbled off to piss in the trees, bludgeoning them and then stealing their swords to slip between the ribs of others. The spine kings feared no one and now they would pay, ambushed in their own village in the midst of their death bacchanal. Sick with images of brutal murder, keyed to the highest pitch of tension, Thel leaped to his feet involuntarily as a crash and cries came from the direction of the beach, and the guards in the clearing's hut rushed out and down a path. "The platform!" someone was shouting in the distance as Thel ran to the bonfire and snatched up a brand. Sparks streamed in a wide arc from the burning end as he ran to the cage and crushed the red ember tip against the lashings at the bottom of a pole. This cage was better constructed and it was going to take longer. A twig cracked behind him and the swimmer croaked a warning; he swung the brand around and caught an onrushing guard in the face. The guard's raised broadsword flew into the cage, cutting one prisoner who cried out; the guard himself couldn't do more than grunt, as Thel beat him furiously across the neck and head. When Thel turned back to the cage the prisoners had cut the lashing with the sword and were squeezing out of the cage and cursing one another under their breath. Thel took the swimmer woman by the arm and pulled her out; she was thicker than the others and barely fit through the gap. She appeared dazed, but when Thel held her face in his hands and caught her eye, she recognized him. Garth had reappeared, and Thel was about to lead the swimmer out of the clearing when one of the other prisoners said urgently, "Wonderful saviours, thank you eternally, please, follow me, I know where the trailhead is that leads up to the spine!" So they followed him, but it seemed to Thel he went straight for the center of the camp.

Shrieks cut the night and torches had been tossed high into the trees, some of which had caught fire and become great torches themselves, so that there was far too much light for their purpose. "Wait one moment please," the prisoner who claimed to know the way said, and he ran into the largest house in the camp.

Apparently some of the treefolk amputees had found the flex X and set it alight. The crater wall enclosing the lagoon appeared out of the darkness, faintly illuminated by the burning village. Sparks wafted among the stars, it seemed the cosmos was winking out fire by fire. The prisoner ran out of the house carrying a sack. "Follow me now," he cried jubilantly, "and run for your lives!"

They ran after him. Thel took the swimmer by the arm, determined not to lose her in the mayhem. But now the prisoner was true to his word, and he led them through firebroken shadows to a wide cobbled trail, ignoring the shouts and cries around them. The trail ran up to the crater's rim and then along it, to the point where the crater wall diverged from the great slope of the spine ridge. The trail began to switchback up the slope. Looking across an arc of the lagoon they saw the village dotted with burning trees and smaller patches of fire, the flex X burning high on a beach glossy as a seal's back, and there were two images of everything: one burning whitely over the beach, another, inverted, burning a clear yellow in the calm black water of the bay.

EIGHT

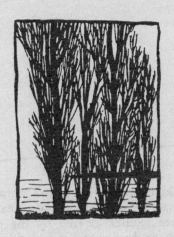

THE
MIRROR

Afraid of the spine king's pursuit, they ran the trail west for many days, scarcely pausing to loot caches located by the prisoner who led them. The caches contained clothing and shoes, and also buried jugs of dried meat and fruit, lumps so hard and dry they couldn't tell what anything was until chewing it; good food, but because there were seven of them they were still hungry. "We'll come to my village soon," the prisoner said one evening after doling out a meager dinner, and outfitting Thel and the swimmer in pants and tunics, and boots that were a lucky fit. The prisoner's name was Tinou, and he had a wonderful big smile; he seemed astonished and delighted to have escaped the spine kings, and often he thanked Thel and Garth for their rescue. "When we get there we'll eat like the lords of the ocean deep."

The sun had set an hour before, and a line of clouds over the western horizon was the pink of azaleas, set in a sky the color of lapis. The seven sat around a small fire: Thel, the swimmer, Garth, Tinou, and three women. These women all had faces cast in the same mold, and a strange mold it was; where their right eye should have been the skin bulged out into another, smaller face, lively and animated, with features that did not look like the larger one around it—except for the fact that its own little right eye was again replaced by a face, a very little face—which had an even tinier face where its right eye should have been, and so on and so on, down in a short curve to the limit of visibility, and no doubt beyond.

This oddity made the three women's faces impressive and even frightening, and because the three full-sized faces seldom spoke, Thel always felt that when talking to them he was really conversing with one of the smaller faces—perhaps the very smallest, beyond the limit of visibility—who might reply in a tiny high squeak at any time.

But now the three women stood before Tinou, and one said, "We want to know what you took from Kataptron Cove."

"I took this bag," Tinou said, "and it's mine."

"It is all of ours," the middle woman said, her voice heavy and slow. Her companions moved to Tinou's sides. "Show us what it is."

In the dusk it was hard to tell if expressions or firelight were flickering across Tinou's long and mobile face. Thel and the swimmer leaned forward together to see better this small confrontation, and Tinou flashed them his friendly smile. "I suppose there is justice in that," he said, and picked up his shoulder bag. Untying the drawstring he said, "Here," and slipped something out of the bag, a small shiny plate of some sort.

"Gold," the middle facewoman said.

Tinou nodded. "Yes, in a manner of speaking. But it is more than that, in fact. It is a mirror, see?"

He held it up—a round smooth mirror with no rim, the glass of it golden rather than silver. Held up against the dark eastern sky it gleamed like a lamp, revealing a rich blue line in a field of pink.

"It is no ordinary mirror," Tinou said. "My people will reward us generously when we arrive with it, I assure you."

He put it back in the bag, and for a moment it seemed to Thel he was stuffing light into the bag as well, until with a hard jerk he closed the drawstring. Wind riffled over them, below lay the calm surface of the sea, and in the east the moon rose, its blasted face round and brilliant; looking from it to the quick yellow banners of their fire, Thel suddenly felt he walked in a world of riches. Night beach and big-handed children, running the mirrorflake road on the sea. . . .

The next dawn they were off again. At first Thel had been shy of the swimmer, even a bit frightened of her; she couldn't know how important her image had been to him before the rescue, and he didn't know what to say to her. But now he walked behind her or beside her, depending on the width of the trail, and as they walked he asked her questions. Who was she? What did she remember from before the night they had washed onto the beach? What had gotten them to that point under the water? What was her name?

She only shook her head. She remembered the night on the beach; beyond that she was unable to say. She concentrated her gaze on her long feet, which seemed to have trouble negotiating the rock, and rarely looked at him. He didn't mind. It was a comfort to be walking with her and to know that someone shared the mystery of his arrival on the peninsula. She was a fellow exile, moving like a dancer caught in heavier gravity than she was used to, and it was a pleasure just to watch her as the sun roasted her brown hair white at the tips, and burned her pale skin red-brown. Often aspects of her reminded Thel of that first night: the set of her rangy shoulders, the profile of her long nose. With speech or without, she reassured him.

And Garth—Garth too was an exile, a new one, and he hiked with them but in himself, skittish, distracted, sad. Thel hiked with him as well, and told him more stories of the rock under their feet, and Garth nodded to show he was listening; but he wasn't entirely there. The leaves on his little tree drooped, as if they needed watering.

So they moved westward, and the peninsula got steep and narrow again, the granite as hard as iron and a gray near black, flecked with rose quartz nodules. The dropoffs on both sides became so extreme that they could see nothing but a short curved slope of rock, and then ocean, a few thousand feet below. Tinou told them that here the walls of the sea cliffs were concave, so that they walked on a tube of rock that rested on a thin vertical sheet of stone, layered like an onion. "Exfoliating granite," Thel said. Tinou nodded, interested, and went on to say that in places the two cliffsides had fallen away to nothing, so that they were walking on arches over open holes, called the Serpent's Gates. "If you were on the tide trail, you could climb up into them and sit under a giant rainbow of stone, the wind howling through the hole."

Instead they tramped a trail set right down the edge of a fishback ridge. In places the trail had been hacked waist-deep into the dense dark rock, to give some protection from falls. Every day Tinou said they were getting close to his village, and to support the claim (for somehow his cheerful assurances made Thel doubt him), the trail changed under their feet, shifting imperceptibly from barely touched broken rock to a loose riprap, and then to cobblestones set in rings of concentric overlapping arcs, and finally, early one morning shortly after they started off, to a smoothly laid mosaic, made of small polished segments of the rose quartz. Longer swirls of dark hornblende were set into this pink road, forming letters in a cursive alphabet, and Tinou sang out the words they spelled in a jubilant tenor, the "Song of Mystic Arrival in Oia" as he explained, fluid syllables like the sound of a beach stream's highest gurgling. At one point for their benefit he sang in the language they all shared:

> *We walk the edge of pain and death*
> *And carve in waves our only hearth*
> *And nothing ever brings us home*
>
> *But something makes us want to climb:*
> *The sight of water cut like stone*
> *A village hanging in the sky.*
>
> *A village hanging in the sky*
> *And nothing ever brings us home*
> *But something makes us climb.*

And climb they did, all that long day, until they came over a rise in the ridge, and there facing the southern sea, tucked in a steep scoop in the top of the cliff, was a cluster of whitewashed blocky buildings, lined in tight rows so that the narrow lanes were protected from the wind. Terrace after terrace cut the incurved slope, until it reached an escarpment hanging over the sea; from there a white staircase zigzagged down a gully to a tiny harbor below, three white buildings and a dock, gleaming like a pendant hanging from Oia.

NINE

THE
SORCERERS OF
OIA

A crowd greeted them as they entered the village, men and women convening almost as though by coincidence, as though if Tinou and his retinue had not appeared they would have gathered anyway; but when they saw Tinou they smiled, for the most part, and congratulated him on his return. "Not many escape the spine kings," one woman said, and laughing the others crushed in on them to touch Tinou and his companions, while Tinou sang the trail's mosaic song, ending with an exuberant leap in the air.

"I thought I would never return here again," he cried, "and I never would have if not for Thel here, who slipped into the spine king's village the night we were to be torn apart on the crossing trees. He set us free, he saved our lives!" Jubilantly he embraced Thel, then added, "He made it possible for all of us to return to Oia—" and he took the mirror out of his shoulder bag.

Silence fell, and the crowd seemed both to step back and to press in at once. Thel thought he could hear the sound of the sea, murmuring far below. A woman dressed in a saffron dress said, "Well, Tinou, your return was one thing, but *this* — "

General laughter, and then they were being led into the narrow streets of the village. These either contoured across town, making simple arcs, or ascended it in steep marble staircases, each step bowed in the middle from centuries of wear. Every lane and alley was lined by blocky whitewashed buildings, often painted with the graceful cursive lettering. By the time they came to a tiny plaza on the far side of the village, the sun was low on the horizon, it broke under clouds and suddenly every west wall was as gold as Tinou's mirror, and many of the west-facing windows were blinding white.

Restaurants ringed the plaza, each sporting a cluster of outdoor tables, and as dusk seeped into things lanterns were hung in small gnarled trees or put on windowsills, and the people ate and drank long into the night. Thel and the swimmer and the three facewomen ate voraciously, and became drunk on the fiery spirits poured for them, and the villagers danced, their long pantaloons and dresses swirling like the colors in a kaleidoscope, yards of cloth spinning under strong wiry naked torsos, both men and women dancing like gods, so that the watchers were shocked when a bottle shattered and the color of blood spurted into their field of vision, off to the side; a fight, quickly broken up, overridden by the gaiety of the sorcerers of Oia. The mirror was back.

In the days that followed, the celebration continued. Eventually it became clear that this was the permanent state of things in Oia, that this was the way the sorcerers lived. They poured sea water into stone vats, and later drew their spirits from taps at the vats' bottoms. Sea lions brought them their daily fish in exchange for drinks of this liquor; the creatures swam right up to the dock at the cliff bottom, barking hoarsely as they deposited long three-eyed fish on the dock. Later the sorcerers turned some of the fish meat into tough dark red steak, which tasted nothing like the flaking fish. Their gardens and goats were tended by their children—and in short, they lived lives of leisure, playing complex games, undergoing abstruse studies, and performing rituals and ceremonies. Tinou took his fellow travelers with him wherever he went, and introduced them as his saviours, and they were fêted to exhaustion.

One day to escape it Thel and the swimmer walked down the staircase trail that switchbacked precipitously to the sea. On the way they passed grown-over foundations, and roofless walls filled with weeds: vestiges of earlier Oias, shaken by earthquakes into the sea. On the dock below some of the sorcerers stood talking to the sea lions, taking their bloody catch and pouring tankards of the liquor down their throats. Even their vilest imprecations couldn't keep a flock of gulls away, and the gulls wheeled overhead crying madly until the barking sea lions breached far into the air, thick sleek sluglike bodies twisting adroitly as they snagged birds and crushed them in their small powerful mouths. Eventually the gulls departed and the lions swam off, a wrack of feathered corpses left on the groundswell.

After they were gone, Thel and the swimmer shed their garments and dove in. Underwater Thel became instantly afraid, but the sight of the swimmer stroking downward was somehow familiar, and strangely reassuring. He stayed under for as long as he could hold his breath, and then joined her in body-surfing the groundswells that rose up to strike the cliffs. As the two rode the waves they remained completely inside the water, surfing as the sea lions did, and they were drawn swiftly forward in the wave until they ducked down and out to avoid crashing into the cliff or the dock. During these rides, slung through the water by two curves of spacetime rushing across each other, Thel would look over at the swimmer's long naked body and feel his own flowing in the water, until it was hard to hold his breath, not because he was winded but because he needed to shout for joy.

When they pulled themselves back onto the worn stones of the dock, Tinou was there, except now he was a woman, laughing in a contralto at their expressions as she stripped and dove in; her face was clearly Tinou's, unmistakable despite the fact that it was slimmer, more feminine—yet clearly not a sister or twin, no, nothing but Tinou himself, shape-changed into a svelte female form. Thel and the swimmer looked at each other, baffled by this transformation; and halfway through the long climb up the stairs Tinou caught up with them, a man again, coquettishly embracing first the swimmer and then Thel (slim wet arms quick around his shoulders), and then laughing uproariously at their expressions.

That sunset he led them and the facewomen down into the ruins of the previous village. Here broken buildings had dropped their barrel roofs onto their floors, and worn splintered sticks of old furniture still stuck out between the bowed bricks. Other sorcerers set lanterns in a circle around what appeared to be an abandoned plaza, smaller even than the one above, and in the long lavender dusk more of the sorcerers gathered, somber for once and drinking hard. In the sky above a windhover caught the last rays of the sun, a white kestrel turned pink by the sunset, fluttering its wings in the rapid complex pattern that allows it to stay fixed in the air.

Tinou took the stolen mirror from his bag and set it on a short wooden stand, on the eastern edge of the circle the sorcerers made. Against the starry east it was a circle of pure pink sheen. When Tinou sat down the circle of seated sorcerers was complete, and they began to sing, their faces upturned to the windhover riding the last rays of the sun. The light leaked out of the sky and the wind riffled the enormous space of dusk and the sea, and Thel, surprising himself, feeling the old compulsion, said, "As you can change your shape, and bend the world to serve you, perhaps you can tell me how this world came to be the way it is."

They all stared at him. "We have only a story," Tinou said finally in a kind tone, "just like anyone else."

Another voice took over, that of an old woman; but it was impossible to pick out the speaker from the circle of faces. "The universe burst from a bubble the size of an eye, some fifteen billion years ago, and it has been flying apart ever since. It will achieve its maximum reach outward in our lifetimes, and fall back into that eye of density which is God's eye, and then all will begin again, just as it was the time before, and the time before that, eternally. So that every breath that you take has occurred in just that way an infinity of times, and none of us are but statues in time to the eye of God."

"As for this world," said the voice of an old man, a cold, hard voice, "this road of mountain across an empty sea, an equatorial peninsula circumnavigating the great globe: it came about like this.

"Gods fly through space in bubbles of glass, and their powers exceed ours as ours exceed those of the stones we stand on, who know only to endure. And once long ago gods voyaged through this forgotten bay of the night sea, and to pass the time they argued a point of philosophy." And here the speaker's voice grew harsh, the edge of every word sharper, until they were as edged as the taste of Garth's shoulder fruit, sending the same kind of bitter shock through Thel. "They argued aesthetics, the most metaphysical of philosophical problems. One of them said that beauty was a quality of the universe independent of any other, that it was inlaid in the fabric of being like gravity, in a pattern that no one could pull out. Another disagreed: beauty is the ache of mortality, this god said, an attribute of consciousness, and nothing is beautiful except perceived through the love of lost time, so that wherever there is beauty, love was there also, and first."

Here another voice spoke, on the breaking edge of bitterness. "And so they agreed to put it to a test, and being gods and therefore just like us, less ignorant but no less cruel, they decided to transform and populate one of the planets they sailed by, sinking all its land but this spine under an endless sea, and then making what remained as beautiful as they could imagine; but leeching every living thing of love, to see if the beauty would yet remain. And here we are."

Silence. For a moment Thel felt he was falling.

A tray was passed around, and Thel did as the rest and took from it a thin white wafer, feeling a powerful compulsion. He ate it and his skin tingled as if crystallizing. Looking up he thought he could still see the kestrel hovering overhead, a black star among the sparkling white ones. The mirror's surface was a dark lustrous violet now, nothing like the western sky which had grown as dark as the east; as his gaze began to fall into the drop of rich glossy color there was a disturbance across the circle, and one of the sorcerer children burst among them. "The spine kings," she gasped, "at the Thera Gate."

All the sorcerers rose to their feet.

"So," Tinou said, "we must hurry a little."

Quickly several of them seized Thel by the arms and legs; when he struggled he might as well have been thrashing on an iron rack. His skin was shattering. The swimmer and the three facewomen were being held back. Thel was lifted up, carried to the mirror.

Tinou appeared beside him, touched his temple. His smile was solicitous. "My thanks for the rescue," he said jovially, then in more formal tones: "Through mirrors we see things right way round at last."

They shoved his left foot into the surface, which was as smooth as a glass of water full over the rim, completely violet and completely gold at one and the same time; and the foot went in to the ankle. Now he had a left foot made of fire, it seemed, and he twisted in the implacable grip, cried out. Tinou nodded sympathetically, cocked his head. "It's pain most proves we live. Nothing serves better to focus our attention on our bodies and the flesh metronomes ticking inside them, timing the bombs that will go off some day and end the universe. Remember!"

He stepped forward and leaned over Thel's face, looked at him curiously. "There are so many kinds of pain, really." They shoved his leg in to the hip. "Is it pulsing, throbbing, shooting, lancing, cutting, stabbing, scalding? Is it pressing, gnawing, cramping, wrenching, burning, searing, ripping? Is it smarting, stinging, pricking, pounding, itching, freezing, drilling? Is it superficial or profound? Can you think of anything else? Can you tell me what eight times six equals? Can you take a full breath and hold it?"

And with each question Thel was thrust further in. A brief flare of genitals, the sickening twist of the gut, all his skin an organ of pain, every atom of him spinning in vain efforts to fly off—and Tinou, smiling, leaning over his face and questioning still, each word slower, louder, more drawn out: "Is it dull, sore, taut, tender? Is it rasping, splitting, exhausting, sickening? Is it suffocating, frightful, punishing? Vicious, wretched? Blinding? Horrible? Killing? Excruciating? Unbearable?"

Then they got his face to the glossy surface, and the reflected visage within was that of a complete stranger, puffy and thick-necked, eyes bulging out—"I have never looked like that," Thel tried to say, certain he was dying. Compared to this the flex X would have been bliss, he thought, and with one last glimpse of Tinou's laughing face he was through the glass and gone.

TEN

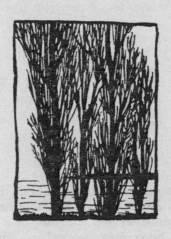

THROUGH THE
MIRROR

Blue stars ahead, red behind. Flare of an oil lamp in the library. We know more than our senses ever tell us, but how? How? Old brown globe, bookcases, beyond it a glassine sphere, the image of a wall. Milky black of the galactic core, tumbling down, down, down, down. Emergency landing. Emergence. The sensuous rise to consciousness.

Splayed on riprap, the taste of ocean wrack in his throat. Once with his parents he tripped and smashed his nose, vivid image of sunny pain and a chocolate ice cream, down by the canals filled with trash, a glassy sheen like the taste of blood suffusing every sun-drenched manifestation of the world. Filled with sudden grief at the lost past, Thel sat up shakily and wiped his nose, spat red. Bloody spit on uneven paving stones, crowded with dead weeds. The whole village of Oia was in ruins, the walls just a block or two high. Dark wind was keening through him and the weeds rustled, it had been centuries and clearly he would never see the swimmer on the night beach again, it was past and irrecoverable. All his past was gone for good even if he could remember it; given the sense of loss for what little he could remember, it was perhaps for the best that so much was forgotten. But he knew he had had a life, childhood, adolescence, he felt its intensity and knew it would never return no matter what he did, even if he remembered every instant of it perfectly, as he felt he did, all of it right there behind some impermeable membrane in his mind, pressing against his thoughts until the ache of it filled everything.

And yet really it didn't matter if he remembered or not. Live a life and seize it to you with an infant's fierce clench of the fist, it still would slip away as lovely as the mountain sky at dusk and *never come back again:* not the moment in the dim library, the noon by the poolside, that moonlit beach and the warm sandy touch, none of it, none of it, none of it. How he loved his past in that moment, how he wanted it back! Eternal recurrence, as the sorcerers had said; ah, it would almost be worth it to be a clockwork mechanism, a bronze creature of destiny, if you could then have it over and over and over. As long as it felt new at every recurrence, who cared? He was a creature of destiny in any case, impelled by forces utterly beyond his control. To move his forefinger left rather than right was an enormous exertion against fate, anything more was too much to ask, it would be only water splashing uphill for a moment; he would bend to the curve of spacetime at last, which leads to the sea in the end. Fate is the path of least action. And if you never know it is all recurrence then it only means you feel the loss, over and over and over. But he had loved his life, he knew he had, the bad and the good and he wanted to keep it forever, all of it, to observe it from some eternal beach and perhaps step back into it, a moment here, a moment there, looking out a bay window at streetlight, bare branch, falling snow, listening to a snatch of piano by the coals of a fire, those moments of being when all the past seemed in him and alive, suffusing the moment and the only moment with a feeling—with every feeling, all at once.

Wind soughed in the weeds. Inside him the flesh metronome went tick, tick. Life slipped away hadron by hadron, limning every joy with a rime of grief; and he walked backward into the future, waving and crying out "Good-bye! Good-bye! Good-bye!"

It was dark. There were only pinprick stars, a dozen at most though the sky was black as an eye's pupil. Shivering with fear, he stood and staggered up one of the marble staircases, now littered with blocks of stone which glowed whitely underfoot, apparently from some internal luminance, so faint it was at the edge of the visible. He was seeing the skeleton of the world.

On the spine the view of both seas was disorienting, literally in that he became aware that the sun would dawn in the west, and that he would have to trek east to new ground to escape the spine kings. Still it was reassuring to see both the oceans, to straddle the high edge of the peninsula, riding the back of the present as it snaked through past and future. He stood there for a minute, savoring the view and the bitter bite of the wind.

Looking back down at the dark luminous ruins of Oia, he saw a figure moving up terrace after terrace, flitting between walls and seeming at times to jump from place to place instantaneously. The figure looked up, and its eyes gleamed like two stars in its dark face. Thel shivered and waited, knowing the figure was coming to join him; and so it did, taking much of the night though it moved rapidly.

Finally it approached him: a man, though it was

a man so slight and fluid in his movement that he seemed androgynous, or feminine. His skin was blacker than the sky, so that his smile and the whites of his eyes seemed disembodied above clothing that glowed like the stones of Oia, outlining his slim form. "The spine kings are upon us," he said in a bright, friendly voice. "Sidestepping them only works for so long. If you want to escape you'll have to move fast. I can show you the way."

"Lead on," Thel said. He knew he could trust this figure, at the same time that another part of his mind was aware that it was a manifestation of Tinou. The intonation of the voice was the same, but it didn't matter. This one could be trusted. "What is your name?" Thel asked, to be sure.

"I am Naousa," the figure said, and reached forward in a confidential way to touch Thel lightly on the upper arm, a touch suasive and erotic. "This way."

He led Thel to a steep drop-off in the ridge, unlike anything Thel had seen before. Here the spine of the peninsula planed down and away in a smooth flat incline, as if an enormous blade had shaved off the mountain range, cutting at a hard angle down toward the beaches. Cliffs on the sides to north and south remained, while the cut itself descended at nearly a forty-five-degree angle. The exposed stone of the cut was as smooth as glass, and a black that somehow indicated it would be dark gray in daylight. Descending this slippery slope would be extremely difficult on foot, but Naousa reached deep into a cleft in the granite and pulled out two lightweight bobsleds, both a whitish color. The sleds' bottoms were smoother than the glassy rock slope, and had no runners or steering mechanism. "You lean in the direction you want to go," Naousa said. "The drop isn't entirely level left to right, so you have to steer a little to keep from going over the cliffs. Just follow me, and look out for bumps." And before Thel could nod he had jumped on his bobsled and was off.

Thel threw his sled down and sat on it, and quickly was sliding down the slope. Naousa was an obvious dot below, cutting big slalom curves down an invisible course. The cut slope was only a couple hundred feet wide, though it broadened as they dropped lower. Bumps and curves invisible to the eye threw Thel left and right as he picked up speed, accelerating at what seemed an accelerating rate; he realized the only hope for survival was to follow Naousa's every move, even if it meant going as fast as Naousa and staying right on his tail. Naousa was flying down the slope, carving wide curves and crying out for joy— Thel could hear the shouts wafting back at him as another impossible turn by Naousa skirted the cliffs. It was thrilling to watch and Thel shouted himself, leaning hard left or right to follow Naousa's bold track, and despite the fact that it was like bobsledding on an open ice slope with cliffs on both sides, Thel began to enjoy himself—to enjoy the contemplation of Naousa's expertise, and his own reproduction of it, and the sheer noise of the sleds and the wind smashing his face and the tears streaming back over his ears and off the cliff edges into space, falling down like dewdrop stars into the original salt.

It was a long ride but did not take much time. At the bottom they sledded out onto the grass of a meadow and tumbled head over heels. Naousa picked up the sleds and tucked them behind a round boulder perched on the ridge. Down here the peninsula was different in character: the stone old and weathered and graying, the spine only fifty to a hundred feet above the noisy sea, and the beaches to both sides wide, with sand white as could be, even in the starless night. "The south side is the easiest walking," Naousa said, and headed down to the north side.

Thel shouted thanks, and dropped to the south side, and walked west toward the sunrise. The sun would be up soon, the sky to the west was blueing. The white sand underfoot was tightly packed; scuffing it made a squeaking sound, *squick, squick*, and the scuffed sand sprayed ahead of Thel's feet in brief blazes of phosphorus. The dunes behind the tidal stretch were neatly scalloped, and covered with dense short grass all blown flat, pointing west to the dawn. The dome of the sky was higher down here and fuzzier, the blues of dawn glowing pastels. Then as he walked stars began popping into sight overhead and he stepped knee deep into the beach, as if the sand were gel; he was sinking in it, the sky was the pink of cherry blossoms and he was in sand to his cheekbones, drowning in it.

ELEVEN

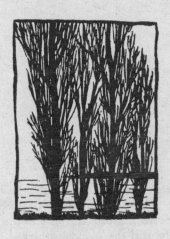

INSIDE THE
WAVE

The sun was hot on his cheek. There was too much light. He rolled on sand, shaded his eyes with a hand and cracked a lid: his brain pulsed painfully and the eyelash-blurred gold-on-white pattern meant nothing to him, then coalesced with a jolt that jerked his body up. The swimmer lay on the wide morning beach. Beyond her lay Garth and the three facewomen, leaves in their hair and long scratches on their arms and legs. Then he saw the shape of the mirror, in a bag tucked under the swimmer's outstretched arm. He was sitting and he almost rolled to her side, every muscle creaking as if carved of wood. He shook her arm, afraid to touch the bag holding the mirror.

She woke, and he asked her what had happened. She stared at him.

"I don't remember," he explained. "I mean, Tinou and the others pushed me through that," pointing at the mirror bag. "After that . . ."

She spoke slowly. "The spine kings attacked and everything caught fire. The sorcerers left you on the plaza, and the mirror as well. We picked you up and carried you away, and took the mirror too. Then you woke and told us to follow you, and we did. We climbed out on the cliff face beside Oia to escape the sorcerers and the spine kings, and the next night we climbed to the spine and started west. You talked most of the time but we couldn't see who you talked to. Garth carried the mirror. The spine dropped into a forest and you ran all the way, and we chased you. Then it seemed you were never going to see us, and so Garth said we should push you back through the mirror. We did that and you fell through, unconscious—"

"You could just push me through?"

"No, it wouldn't work at first, it was hard as glass when I tried it, but Garth said it had to be at sunset, on the spine, with a kessel hawk hunting in the western sky. We waited three days until we saw one, and then it worked. But after we got you through you were asleep again. So we waited and then we fell asleep too. I'm hungry."

The others were stirring at the sound of their voices. They woke and the beach air was filled with the chatter of voices over the hiss of broken waves. As they shared their stories they walked to the sea without volition, drawn by their hunger. The peninsula had changed to something like what Thel had traversed in his time beyond the mirror: a low forested mound snaking through the sea, sandy moon bays alternating with chalky headlands. They walked to the next bay, which faced north. Here the beach was a steep pebbly shingle that roared and grumbled at every wave's swift attack and retreat, and among the millions of shifting oval pebbles, which when wet looked like semiprecious stones, they found crabs, beach eels, scraps of seaweed that the facewomen declared edible, and one surprised-looking fish, tossed up by a wave and snatched by Garth. As they made their catch they wandered west, marking the sine curve of the hours with their passage until the sun was low. Knobs of old worn sandstone stood here and there like vertebrae out of the scrubby forest, and they climbed to one of these bony boulder knots collecting dead wood as they went, and in the sunset made a fire using Garth's firestone and knocker. Every scrap of the sea's provender tasted better than the last, the least scrap finer than a master chef's creation. Clouds came in from the south as if a roll of carpet had been kicked over them, and the sinking sun tinted the frilly undersurface a delicate yellow. Their fire blazed through the long dusk, and in the wind the whitecaps tossed, so that it felt like they were on the deck of a ship.

Each day they foraged west, and spent the night on knolls. "We'll reach your folk soon?" Thel asked the facewomen.

"No. Many days. But when we do, you can continue on your way speeded by our horses."

They hurried on, their hunger not quite held in check by the wrack of the waves. The peninsula straightened, and looking back they could see the big curve of land rising to the great ridge of Oia. Ahead of them the spit seemed, judging from the high points, to continue its gentle rise and fall indefinitely. They hiked on the beaches, over wet round stones that clacked together all the day long. Thel and the swimmer dove into the waist-high shore break more than once, ostensibly to try to catch briefly glimpsed fish, but really just for the feel of the dive and the wave's dizzying lift. In the evenings around the fire they pulled the mirror from its bag and contemplated it cautiously. Each of them saw different things in it, and they couldn't agree on its color. Salmon, gold, copper, lapis; such divergence of perception was frightening, and they snapped at each other and put it away, and slept uneasily.

One dawn Thel woke. The night before the mirror had been left face up on a rock, and he circled his hand over it, looking down at eyes, hair, red stones, years. The swimmer inched over the sandstone and lay prone beside him, their heads together as they peered down into it, as if looking down a well. "What is it?" Thel said.

"It shows the truth," the swimmer said, then smiled. "Or maybe it just makes things pretty."

They tilted it so it reflected their two faces.

"Hey!" Thel exclaimed. "That's me."

It was the face he knew from a million beard burns: narrow jaw, round forehead, long nose, wide mouth. He would have looked a long time but the reflection of the swimmer stole his gaze; it was her face, but subtly transformed, the harsh strong lines emphasized and given a pattern, a human face before anything else but so purely human that it was, he thought happily, that of a god.

They broke their gazes at the same time and looked at each other; grinning like children who have gotten away with something forbidden, they let the mirror drop and rolled together. Blood surged through Thel as they kissed and made love, he sank into her as if into a wave, riding inside the wave on an endless rise, pulled along as when body-surfing. Touch was everything then, her skin, the stone under his knees and elbows; but once he looked up and saw the mirror beyond her head and filled with joy he waved a hand over it: gold light flashed up into the chill salt predawn air.

TWELVE

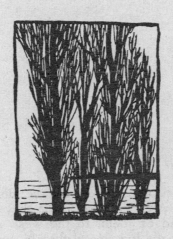

THE
FACEWOMEN

After that Thel carried the mirror bag himself. And the next night they saw bonfires ahead of them, to the west. As they progressed along the low line of the old sandstone ridge, the air thick with salt and the roar of waves, the peninsula took a pronounced swing to the north, making an immense arc thrown in the sea. And to the west where the horizon washed over the black mark of the spit, a short line of bonfires sparked against the late twilight sky. Apparently where these fires burnt the peninsula was quite a bit taller, for the dots of yellow light were a good distance above the obsidian sea; nevertheless they flickered to the point of disappearing briefly from sight. The three facewomen stood and watched intently. "They are our signal beacons," one said, and after a while added, "They say we are being pursued."

So they began to hike all through the long days, and in the dawns and dusks, and each night the three facewomen talked among themselves, and then one night their eyefaces talked among themselves, in high-pitched voices; and yet they said to the other three travelers only, "We are being pursued." Until the distance between the bonfires began to decrease, and the line of four was almost one wide fire, growing brighter from right to left. Then they said, "We are being pursued; but we have almost reached our home."

Wearily they hiked on, spurred by this pronouncement, and slept one more night out, and then the next day in the late morning they came to a deep stone-ringed firepit. The leader of the facewomen crouched and touched one of the stones. "We are home," her eyeface said. She and her two companions led the way thereafter, skipping from knob to knob and touching each fire ring, then running downhill into the next swale between knobs. The peninsula became broader and more verdant: between the bonfire tors the crest ridge split in two broad lines of hilltops, holding between them sunken meadows spotted with vernal ponds that were in this season patches of bright grass strewn with wildflowers, dots of pure color. These meadows, strung like green stones on a necklace, grew larger and larger until they came on one that was broad and flat, and ringed by a split log fence and a number of low twisty pines. At the far side of the fenced-in enclosure clustered a herd of small quick dark horses, flowing along the fence like a single organism. In the trees behind the fence stood hexagonal buildings with wood walls and hide roofs. These were arranged in circles, like their firepits or their corral.

The three facewomen ran to one of the huts and burst into it, and emerged with a small gang of other facewomen clinging to them and shouting. When they had calmed down, Thel, the swimmer, and Garth were welcomed with a fluid formality, recursive smiles of welcome shrinking away into the infinity of the facewomen's right eyes. It seemed to Thel that all the inhabitants of the meadow were women, but he noticed children among them, and saw that they tended to clump in groups of three; Garth confirmed that these were reproductive units.

Their threesome took them to what appeared to be the oldest threesome, village elders who greeted them and thanked them for rescuing their granddaughters. Thel took the opportunity to ask how the bonfire messengers had known they were being pursued.

"We saw the pursuers," one of the threesome said.

Thel frowned. "How?"

They led him to the knob above the village. There in the rocks stood a short pyramid of black fitted stone, holding up a long hollow tube carved from the same stone, set with a thick clear lens at each end.

"A telescope!" Thel said.

The old women nodded. "You know the principle?"

"Yes." Thel waited while one of them aimed the glass, then stooped to look through it. "It's powerful!"

"Yes. More powerful than that, in fact. But that is sufficient to see the spine kings."

So it was; in the pale colors of the image, swimming on the air, Thel saw ant-like soldiers, tramping in a line along the ridge. He looked over the top of the glass and saw it was pointed some halfway along the visible peninsula. "They're far behind."

"They stopped for other business. They will be here in a few days, at their pace. They will certainly come. We saw through the glass what you are carrying, you see. When the spine kings arrive you must not be here. But we will provide you with horses to speed you on your way west, in thanks for helping our daughters. And you may spend two nights here resting."

They slept in a storage hut on piles of woven blankets, feeling so luxurious that they could scarcely get comfortable. The next day they were taken to the big meadow pasture's corral, and introduced to three of the small horses. "These are young ones," the facewoman in charge of the corral told them. "They're wild but they have no habits—they should accept you. Here, you hold their mane and jump on." The horses' hair was the chestnut red of certain fir trees Thel had seen back on the high spine, and their manes, long and rough, felt exactly like handfuls of the trees' hairy fibrous bark: indeed, looking closely at it, he couldn't see any difference. He laughed. Then the small herd in the enclosure bolted and ran around the inside of the fence, all in a mass, their manes and long russet hair flowing behind them as if they were underwater, and he laughed again. "A horse is a fish made of trees," he told the startled swimmer, and leaped on his animal and rode head pressed into the stiff rough red mane, feeling the sea wind course over him as it had during his wild ride on the other side of the mirror. Jerking the animal's head to one side or another influenced its direction, and pulling back on the mane slowed it, as kicking it spurred it on. The corral mistress said as he leaped off, "Ride these until you come to the brough—they can take you no further. Set them free and they will return to us. They know to hide from the spine kings."

"Thanks for your help," Thel said.

One of the smallest visible eyefaces grinned. "With what you are carrying," it said in a small voice, "we want you as far away as possible when the spine kings arrive."

"Ah."

That night they built a massive bonfire, and

when the flames were leaping as high as the treetops and higher, the eldest three facewomen brought the telescope into the clearing and put it on a portable stand, and stood Thel next to the fire, and pointed the glass at him and looked at him through it. Feeling scorched at the back of his neck, he looked into the lens at the leader's face. She had the telescope placed against her eyeface, and in the little curved circle of glass he saw two eyes, blinking as they observed him: her smallest face, no doubt, too small for the naked eye to see. So there was an end to the recession after all, he thought. The ultimate leader of the facewomen, perhaps; and she said in a squeak, "Stand still. Don't blink so much. Look straight into the glass." He did as he was told, almost laughing because it felt like a kind of eye examination. "How far back can you see?" he asked. The bonfire pushed roasted air past him.

"To your birth," the high voice shrilled. "You have been through the mirror and back. You are not from this world. You fell into this world, one night, into the ocean with the seahorses."

"Before that?" Thel asked, finding it suddenly hard to breathe. The clothes on his back were hot.

"A man in a bubble, flying through the stars. Others like you and not like you. When you were a child, you lived by a lake. The lake was circular and had high cliffs surrounding it. One day you tried to climb the steepest cliff, and fell. You hit the water feet first and survived the impact, plunging deep. The water of the lake was said to be bottomless and so when your feet hit a submerged outcropping of the cliff you were astonished, and in that state of panic these moments of your future came to you, intense as any memory, for every vision is a memory, and every memory a vision of a world that never existed until called up in the mind. You saw then your immersion in our ocean, your step through the mirror, your stand before our glass, the fire behind you, all of it seen in that instant. Remember?"

Falling, water in his eyes, the sudden heat at his back. "Yes," Thel said, wondering, looking within frantically to see all he could of that lost lake, his boyhood, his parents, the cat leaping from the table onto the dog, the old man who loved the clouds —

"Everything which we really are and never quite live," the little voice said, and the whole thing snatched itself away from him and he was only aware of the heat on his back and his hair curling. He walked away, out of the telescope's view and into the purple night, feeling his back radiate against the wet salty air. The face of his mother — he snatched at it, lost it. Dune grass flowing like seaweed, rustling against the chewing sound of waves: clouds drifting through the stars. Never to be in anything but the present, trapped in the moment which is always receding, never ours to have and hold — the swimmer came out after him and found him, and he collapsed onto the sand, sat there with an arm around her strong thigh. "I want to be a stone," he said, "a stone man lying on the beach forever, never to think, never to feel the future sifting through me. I want to be a stone."

"It's the same for them," she said.

THIRTEEN

GARTH'S
APPLES

The following morning they woke with the dawn and the facewomen led them to their horses and waved farewell as they rode off. The horses were exuberant with running and galloped over the dunes waving their heads from side to side like blind things, eating the air and snapping at their riders if they were interfered with. So they hung on and rode: Garth's horse led, the swimmer's brought up the rear. Thick white thunderheads grew over the water to the south, and the colors of everything in the long morning light were richer than they remembered them being, the water a dark glassy blue outside jade green shallows, the foam on the breakers as white as the clouds, the dune grass subtle dusty greens, the red barky hair of their horses an irresistible magnet for the eye. The horses ran along the beach until midday, then cantered up onto the dunes and browsed on the sparse grass. The three riders dismounted stiffly and hobbled them, then walked down to the beach to forage for beach food to supplement the little the facewomen had been able to give them. They ate on the beach, returned to the horses and slept, then in the mid-afternoon rode again. They traveled so much faster than they could have on foot that it was hard to grasp: they were already far from the facewomen's meadow, and the horses ran on tirelessly through the long glarey stretches of late afternoon, until at sunset they trotted to a halt and stood in a wind-protected dip between two dunes, browsing easily through the mauve dusk.

They rode like that for days. Each day the peninsula became lower, narrower, more stripped of life. The thick mats of dune grass reduced to occasional patches, the tufts of grass as sparse as the hair on a balding man. Each tuft had been blown in every direction by the winds, creating a perfect circle of smoothed hard sand around it, deepest at the outer edge; the dunes became geometrical worksheets, sine waves covered with circles. One sunset walking in this deeply patterned sand Thel looked down at a tuft of grass and the perfect circle around it, and thought, That is your life: a stalk of living stuff blown in every direction, leaving a brief pattern in sand.

They had emptied the facewomen's bags of food, and went hungry as the beach provided less and less. One morning Garth plucked two of the fruit from his shoulder tree and offered them to Thel and the swimmer. "I can eat grass," he told them. "More grass, more fruit. Really. Please. We can't afford to spend all day on the beach foraging."

Thel said, "If we stopped in the later afternoon instead of at dusk, we could forage more, and you could eat more too." He scuffed dubiously at the tough dune grass, so sharp-edged you could easily cut skin with it. Garth also spent every evening with his feet buried in the sand; presumably more of that would help too, but it was something Garth didn't talk about.

He did agree to the early stops, however, and so every morning after that Thel and the swimmer ate one of his bitter electric shoulder apples, and felt the chemical tang of it course through them. It was wonderful how well the apples satisfied their appetites, how long they could subsist on them. And Garth ate dune grass in the evenings, and spent time with his feet buried in the sand, and got thinner; but the apples continued to bloom on his shoulder tree, tiny fragrant white blossoms giving way to hard green nubs, which grew quickly into edible fruit.

Then as they rode down the endless spit of the peninsula, even the grasses disappeared. They were on a desert shore, beach on both sides of a low mound of dunes; even the horses had to be fed from Garth's tree, and he had to spend the whole of every afternoon with his body stretched out to the sun, and his feet stuck deep in the sand—haggard, exhausted, a small smile playing over his mouth. "I was told tales of this, how one of us could grow enough to sustain his fellows in a time of need. Like having children, they always said, and now I know what they mean." And he looked at them with a gaze they could scarcely return, so filled was it with a kind of amused maternal affection.

Every morning thunderheads billowed up and sidled across the southern sky, but never hit their stretch of the coast, piling up instead against the mountainous spine far behind them. They found pools of water in holes in the sandstone, proof of storms past, but these had grown brackish with beach dew, and the travelers became thirsty as well.

After many days of this deprivation, they saw in the distance ahead a small knob in the peninsula. Dune grasses returned to the central mound, and they came across more pools of water. Days passed and it seemed they would reach the knob the following afternoon for several days running, but it was bigger than they had first thought, and kept receding.

Finally it loomed up, several hundred feet tall, like a sandstone lighthouse. They skirted it on the wide southern beach, and on the other side discovered a most extraordinary thing: the beach stretched out into the blue sea, and got thinner and lower, until it sank under the water. "It's the end!" Thel cried.

"No, no," Garth said. "It's the water gate. I've heard stories about it. Look out there, see that smudge? It's the other cape, where the peninsula proper begins again. In between is a tidal bar. This is the lowest part of the spine, nothing more. At low tide a strip of sand will emerge as fine as any road, and stay above the waves for half the day."

It proved to be true. As the afternoon progressed the beach extended farther into the water, which was racing from north to south in a strong current, breaking whitely in a straight line that divided the sea. This stretch of white foam boiled furiously in a line to the horizon and the distant smudge of the farther cape. Then in a matter of moments, it seemed, the whitewater divided and fell away into two sets of waves rolling in from right and left, leaving a strip of wet gray sand and wet brown rock standing between them. The breakers tumbled in over rocky shallows on both sides, but the bar stood clear of them. And the spine trail extended even here; squarish blocks of water-holed rock had been laid in a path over the bar, making a causeway a foot or two higher than the bar itself. "The horses can't cross that," Garth said. "The rock would tear up their hooves."

"But surely it's more than one tide's walk across?" the swimmer said.

Garth nodded. "Still we must send the horses back, as we said we would." And he kicked and shouted at the horses, threw rocks at them until they cantered off, and circled nervously; then regarded each other and broke for home, flowing down the beach like a school of red fish darting through the sea.

Something moved on the side of the knob and they jumped, turned to look. It was a man the same color as the sandstone, his skin the same grainy dark brown. As he approached they saw he was naked, and that his eyes, his hair, everything was the brown of the rock. In his eyes the color seemed darker, the way the rock did when it was wet.

He stopped before them and said, "I am Birsay the guide. It is more than one tide's walk to cross the brough, as you noted. This is how we do it; there is a rise near the halfway point, and we run to that in one low tide, on a path that I have built. It is just possible, though you get your legs wet. There on the rise I have left several large holed rocks. We tie ropes I have made to those anchors, and as the water rises we rise on it, floated by slings I have made of kelp bladders and wood. The current pushes us out, usually to the south, but we are tied by the ropes to the anchor rocks, and when the tide ebbs, we float down to a landing, and complete the crossing of the brough to the other cape."

"Why have you made these things?" Thel asked. "Why do you do this?"

The sandstone-colored man shrugged. "The peninsula extends around the world, and there is no land but it. And this is the only place in its circumference where the sea has chewed the peninsula down almost to its level. And naturally the peninsula must be passable. Traders come through, and circumnavigators on pilgrimages—believers of more religious persuasions than I'd care to recall. It is simply the natural order of things. The land itself calls forth a guide to sustain that order, and I am the forty-ninth reincarnation of that guide, Birsay."

He led them to a tall cave entrance in the side of the knob, down stone steps to a dry sand floor. Against one wall were circles of coiled rope, made of some sort of animal hair or plantlike fiber—impossible in this world to be sure which, it occurred to Thel as he examined it. It was thick in the hand, and would certainly hold against any current. The floats Birsay had mentioned were there too, made of the big bulbs one saw at the base of kelp tubes, tied by flat cords to a wooden framework that held them under the arms, and around the chest and back. "You spend almost half a day suspended in the tide," Birsay said. "The water is warm, though by the end it doesn't feel so. The bath is good for the skin. Then the distance from the rise to the western cape is not as great as the distance from here to the rise."

The three travelers conferred by eye. Garth said, "When would you have us leave?"

"We've wasted too much of this ebb. And they are getting longer every day now, for twenty more days. The next one will begin in the dark before dawn."

"The next, then," Thel said, and the other two nodded their agreement.

They spent the night in the cave, around a small warm driftwood fire, the twisted shapes of the wood burning in bright flames tinged with blue, green, salmon. What little smoke there was rose through a blowhole in the roof of the cave. The guide fed them broiled conch, seasoned with wild onions and a gingery seaweed, wonderful after their week of subsistence on Garth's bitter apples.

Birsay had a place for everything, and he moved neatly and quickly around the fire, catching its light just as the cave walls did, so that sometimes it was hard to see him. He brought out a tray of black loam for Garth to stick his feet into after the regular meal was done, and with a blush and a grateful look, Garth silently buried his feet in the dirt.

"Do you guide all travelers that appear here?" Thel asked.

"I do."

"You make no distinctions?"

"What do you mean?"

"Those that follow us are murderers, intent on our lives."

"Is that so?" The wet pebble eyes regarded them with interest. "Well, I wish you all speed. I make no distinctions of that kind, no. Good, evil, right, wrong—they are personal matters, shifting from one to the next. These murderers may regard themselves as righteous folk, and you as great criminals perhaps, thieves of something they cherish, perhaps, who knows?" Though he glanced at Thel's mirror bag as if he did know. "How am I to judge? By your stories? By the looks on your faces?" He dismissed the idea with a flip of the hand. "My task is to lead travelers across the low point in the world road. Their purposes, their identity—none of my concern. One winter I led death himself across the brough, you can still see his footprints in the rock where a wave splashed him and he got angry. . . ." And as the firelight played over his face he told them stories of travelers who had passed, men and women and creatures it sometimes took him the burning of a branch to describe. One such had had the legs and waist of a man, his chest then rising up into the rounded and feathered body of a giant eagle. This creature had spoken to him in grim croaks, and after a while Birsay had guessed the truth; it walked across the brough because it had had its wing muscles clipped, so that it could no longer fly. The guide laughed at Thel: "How judge that, eh? How judge that?"

FOURTEEN

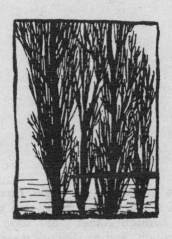

CROSSING
THE BAR

In the middle of the night Birsay crouched by their warm sand beds and roused them. "The brough comes clear soon." They rose and ate more conch, and at Birsay's instruction drank from a jug of fresh water until their stomachs were heavy and cold.

The star flood still lit the beach as they walked onto the wet sand. Birsay watched each wave closely, and as one ran up the sand he pointed. "Last high wave," he said. "From now on they ebb."

Then more and more of the beach was revealed as each wave sluiced back and hopped over the non-existent rail where the water regrouped and turned again. A point emerged, wet tan sand with a cross-hatched stippling of black. Then the waves fell back to left and right as they had the afternoon before, and the line of boiling white water appeared. The bar emerged, at first just as an extension of their point of sand, receding away from them at a walking pace:

then, in the blue of dawn, the water simply ran away from them to right and left, and they walked on a sandbar that extended all the way to the horizon.

Struck silent at the uncanny sight, the three travelers strode quickly after Birsay, their ropes coiled and hung over their shoulders, their floats hanging on straps tied over their own backpacks and bags. The sun rose and cast long faint shadows ahead of them. The seas rolled up flat wet sand to right and left, the northern and southern seas separated only by their spit of wet sand.

They crunched through patches dense with seashells, or squishy with living anemones. It was a blue day, the air clear as glass and the sea and sky darker and lighter shades of the same full blue. The sand and Birsay were a color composed of tan and black sand, mixed thoroughly. A handful of it washed thin by water revealed clear grains, smaller white and brown grains, and tiny floating black flecks.

Then the sand began to grow thin over bedrock of the same color, which broke through as if it were a little model of the spine, here worn to ankle-high knobs and nubs, split by the sea down its grain of stratification, running across the bar from sea to sea. Eventually they walked on bare rock, sharp ribs of brown that ran out under the white waves, which grumbled toward them to nothing in hundreds of parallel grooves. Eventually the shallow faults turned the brough into a stretch of pitted knife edges, set across their way. Walking over these edges would have devastated first sandals and then feet, but Birsay or his predecessors had filled a rough narrow path through the faults with blocks of loose stone—an old path, it seemed, for the blocks were worn in their settings, and in places had been washed away.

They hurried over this low causeway, until when they looked behind they could see no sign of Birsay's knob, or the low peninsula beyond it; ahead they saw no sign of the knob at the halfway point, nor the farther cape. The brough extended all the way to the horizon in both directions, a horizon nearly at eye level, so that it seemed they crossed the bottom of a flattish bowl of ocean, which would sooner or later rush in on them. It was a strange sight.

In late mid-afternoon they came to Birsay's knob, first seen as a bulge in the bar, a widening of the white water to the sides. "We've made good time," Birsay said, "but it's always a close thing. By sunset we'll be floating."

Once on the knob it seemed not much different from the rest of the brough: slightly wider, minutely taller, pocked and runneled like all the rest of the rock they had traversed. In the largest potholes were big blocks of rock that had had holes chiseled through them, and following Birsay's instructions they tied the ends of their ropes through these holes. Birsay chose the anchor rocks very carefully, after observing the surging mush and the wind, and his charges' bodies; he spread them out at intervals along the bar, Thel, Birsay, Garth, the swimmer. Their few possessions they placed in other potholes, with stones placed over them.

They sat on the damp rock, and waited. The tide began to come in.

It was impossible not to be frightened at the sight. Each broken wave rushed at them, at first as thick as the wave had been high, and boiling over the reef below; it thinned as it made its furious rush, until it was bubbling water trickling up the furrows in the rock, and then receding. But each final gurgle was closer than the last.

"Usually the south reaches us first," Birsay said, "because that's where the prevailing winds come from. But today" — he frowned, sniffing — "the wind is from

the east. And the north side is closing faster." He
turned and turned again on the knob's highest point,
sniffing. "It may be windy tonight."

Then, in the surge of just a few waves, the four
of them were sitting on a tiny rock island in a sea of
boiling white water, waves from the two seas running
together and slapping up into the air, in lines of wind-
tossed spray. Then a big wave from the north ran up
the rock and right over their feet and backs. Quicker
than Thel would have believed possible, every wave
rolled over the rock and their lower legs. They stood
around Birsay on the peak, and then waves from the
south sea piled in as well, and up and down the
brough to east and west they could see long sheets of
white water squirting up into the air, underneath them
a chaos of wave and backwash, the sea white with
foam, millions of bubbles hissing out their lives, sending a fine rain into the air and creating a tremendous
loud roar, a roar made of glugs and hisses that individ-
ually would scarcely be heard across a room.

When the water got waist high they were shoved
hard this way and that, and Birsay told them in a loud
voice to hang on—that this was the only tricky part—
and that they should soon cast off and get away from
the knob, trusting to their floats and anchors. When
the waves were chest high they were forced to take his
advice, and they swam off after him to the south, floating easily on their miniature rafts and spreading out as
they were pushed straight out from their anchors.

As the tide rose the water grew calmer, until the
only signs of the brough were long snaking lines of
crusty foam floating away to the south, and an occasional brief mushy break at the top of the largest
waves as they crossed the bar. The waves, and the current that pushed them, were from the northwest. So
they floated to the southeast of the knob, connected to
it like kites flying in the wind of the tidal current. If

they rested they were some thirty feet from each other, and they were about two hundred feet from the submerged knob, so that Thel and the swimmer, on the outsides, could easily paddle over to talk to the middle two. Garth's shoulder tree looked odd indeed sticking up out of the water, like the last remnant of a deluged land. Garth's face was sputtering and apprehensive beside it; he couldn't swim and had to trust his float, clearly a difficult act of faith.

It was a strange sunset. Now the horizon was closer and higher than ever, the dome of the sky taller: all as blue as they had been at dawn. The sun dropped through the air yellow as a daisy and sunk without fanfare, turning green at the end as if the last rays had shone through water. During the long dusk a line of puffy white clouds appeared to the northwest, so tall they redefined the height of the sky. These clouds eventually took on copper and iron hues, and cast their color over everything else, so that the sea took on a coppery sheen, and the air was dark and metallic.

Birsay watched this development nervously, and when the wind shifted and picked up suddenly, he swam to Thel's side and said, "It may be a cold night. The northerlies are hard."

Thel swallowed salt and nodded. Already the water felt warmer than the air, so that his head was cold, and it was warming to duck it into the brine. Birsay said the southern current was warmer still; Thel was content with the northern one, which felt just a touch below body temperature.

But the northwest wind was cold, and the swells rolling by began to steam a little. In the last light of the dusk they saw the line of tall clouds approaching, blocking out the stars that were just popping into salt-blurred existence. The travelers rose and fell on dark swells that steamed whitely. They rose and fell, rose and fell.

The wind strengthened and waves began to break on the bar, emerging from the dark several hundred feet away from them, on the northern shallows. There low dark surges in the sea's surface reared up and toppled over in a white roar, water shattered and tumbling chaotically, in a line as far as they could see. The broken waves rolled over the bar in a low continuous thunder, but as the water deepened again each wave would reconstitute itself out of its own mush, the whitewater shrinking back up the side of the swell until it was only a whitecap; and then it was only a groundswell again, on which they rose and fell, rose and fell, crest to trough and back again.

But the wind got stronger, and the waves bigger. A groundswell breaks when the depth of water below it is equal to the height of the swell, trough to crest; now the swells were as high as the water beneath their feet, and they were at the ends of their ropes, they couldn't get any farther out onto the south sea. The wind picked up again, and now each time they rose on a swell there was broken water at the crest, so that they had to plunge under it and hold their breath until their floats pulled through the wave and out into the air again.

It was raining, Thel noticed once when he came up, a cold rain that roiled the ocean surface and threw up more steam. Now the wind howled, and the waves became big rolling walls of broken white mush, wild and powerful. It was all Thel could do to hold his breath as he was thrashed up and down under these broken waves; he held his float to him, waited grimly each time for it to pull him back up into the roaring black night. When it did he gasped in huge breaths, and looked to his right where the others were, but could see little through the spray. Then another wave would lift him and he would duck under the whitewater, endure its tumbling, come up again. Efforts to swim sideways to Birsay were useless, and getting to Garth and the swimmer unthinkable: and yet she was only ninety feet away.

He could only concentrate on getting under each wave with a full breath, and on staying upright in his float. The night fell into an endless pattern of rising, ducking under whitewater, holding on with lungs bursting, popping back out into the shrieking wind, resting against the float's restraint. Then again. And again. It went on until at one point he got so tired it seemed he couldn't go on, and he considered cutting the rope and floating off to the south on the groundswell. But then a sort of second wind came to him, a stubbornness suffusing every cell of his muscles and lungs, and he worked to make each forced plunge as streamlined and efficient as he could, grimly trying to relax and be at ease as the broken water threw him about, as loose as a rag on a clothesline in a stiff wind. He fell into a rhythm. Nothing marked the passing of time, it seemed he had been breathing in a pattern of submergence in the sea for years. The water began to feel cool, then cold. His head and arms were frigid in the wind's rip.

Then as he floated, waiting for the next rise, lightning forked down to his left. By the fey snap of light he glimpsed dots on the water, heads and floats — and then he was under again. The lightning struck again when he was underwater, he saw the flash and opened his closed eyes and saw a field of bubbles, white in green — then black. Three or four more times lightning struck, but always when he was submerged. He wondered if they would be electrocuted.

Then one wave thumped him down onto rock. The air burst from his lungs and he nearly blacked out before resurfacing. It was still dark night up there, the storm raging, rain coming down harder than ever: he could get a refreshing swallow of fresh water merely by turning his open mouth to the northwest. Submerged again, he kept his feet down and hit the rock bottom more gently. But it got harder as the tide ebbed, and the broken waves swept across the brough more wildly; often they knocked him down against the bottom and thumped him against it repeatedly, until he ached with the battering, and it seemed that after all the night's labors he might be killed by his landing.

Eventually he stood chest high in the waves' troughs, then waist high; but it was too much work to stand, and too cold. He crouched down in the water and let the float and rope hold him, peering through the blackness for the next onrushing wall of whitewater.

Finally the broken waves themselves were low enough that he could float over them, his head clear; and in the troughs the whitewater only sluiced over his knees. He hauled himself up the rope toward the knob, where it was shallower still; he could sit, and turn his back to the waves and the wind. Relaxing his stomach muscles made him retch. When he had gathered some strength he hauled himself up onto the knob, and found the other anchors, and slogged down the length of Garth's rope; out in the murk he could see Garth bobbing.

But it was only his float. "No," Thel said. Rather than return to the knob he just swung on his rope sideways, and bumped into Birsay unexpectedly; but Birsay hung in his float, head back, mouth and eyes wide open to the waves. He had drowned.

Stomach spasming, Thel swung back the other way, stepping on sharp rock. No sign of the swimmer. Back, forth, up, back; nothing. He had to walk back to the knob and find her anchor. The rope hung loose in the water, trailing out to sea, and he hauled it in feeling like Death the Fisherman, afraid and sick at heart. Its end came to him, frayed. In the first predawn blue he peered at the ends of the fibers; it looked like she had chewed through the rope, bitten her way free. The swimmer. He kneeled on the rock, collapsing around his cramped stomach. The swimmer. She had freed herself but kept the float, smart woman. Perhaps she had swum over and pulled Garth from his float, yes. Took them both off the bar, off to where the groundswell would pose no challenge to her swimming powers. Yes. She would come back. Or else swim to the cape in the west.

When dawn illuminated the seascape the tide had ebbed and the brough had returned, thought it was often overrun by the storm surf. Everything today was green, the sea a light jade color, the clouds a heavy dark gray tinged with green, the bar brown, but greenish as if with algae.

Thel untied the float from his chest and tossed it aside. Angrily he kicked Birsay's anchor, left him bobbing in the waves. He put his bags over his shoulder, the mirror like a heavy plate in its wet sack. He took off along the bar, squish squish.

It was hard to walk. Often he got off Birsay's path and fell in knee-deep transverse crevices, cracking his shins so hard that the world itself burst with pain, as it had when he was shoved through the mirror. The wind keened across the brough, in his ear and cold. It rained intermittently and clouds rushed overhead like the horses of the facewomen. Several times he heard the swimmer and Garth calling to him from the surf to his left, but he never saw them. The current in the southern sea was running swiftly toward the cape to the west, which now appeared as a dark hill in the clouds. A good sign, it would help them along. He drank sea water, he was so thirsty; he drank the blood from his shins for food, cupping it in a palm and getting a good mouthful after every fall. Its taste re-

minded him of Garth's fruit. Blindly he kicked on, and
then the brough was sand. He ate some of it. The mirror was heavy on his back, he wanted to toss it aside
but didn't.

He lay on the cape beach, in wet sand. Sand
crabs hopped around him, tried to eat him and he ate
them in return. Along the southern side of the cape,
that was where they would land. A beach stream,
fresh water cutting through the shingle. He lay in it
and drank. When he woke again he was stronger, and
could bury himself in the sand and sleep properly. The
next day he found abalone studding a beach reef like
geodes, and he broke them with rocks and ate the
muscles after pounding them tender. That and the
beach stream infused him with strength, and he began
walking the cape's broad southern beach, under the
steep green prow of the reemerging peninsula. The
beach was studded with pools of water blue as the sky,
and with driftwood logs from what had been immense
trees, and with shell fragments that were sometimes
big enough to sit in. All kinds of debris, on fine tawny
sand, loose underfoot so that he often stumbled, and
sometimes fell.

All kinds of debris: and yet when he came across
one piece of driftwood, he knew it instantly. It was the
remains of a shrub, stripped of leaves and bark—a
thin trunk dividing into thinner branches, their broken
ends rounded and smooth as if rolled in the waves for
years. Just a sand-colored piece of driftwood, a splay
of branches like a hand reaching out. He sat on the
sand and wept.

FIFTEEN

SUBMERGENCE

He wandered the beaches on the southern side of the cape, and during each low tide ventured back out on the brough, looking for signs of the swimmer. In the evenings he grubbed on a beach of oval flat stones for crabs, and cracked more abalone, and felt a traitor to Garth and the swimmer every time he swallowed. He hated his hunger then, the way it drove him, the way he was its slave. The days were so long. During one he sat in the sand at the tip of the cape, on the edge of the prow that rose out of the sea to a grassy peak some five hundred feet above; and each part of that day passed like a year of grieving.

The next day he climbed the grassy peak. When he reached the top he could see far over the brough, a dark swath in the sea studded with whitecaps. It was an overcast day, the sun a white smeary blob and the sky like the inside of an abalone shell, arched over a sea of lead. The brough seemed to disappear out at the horizon, with no sign of the peninsula on the other side, as if the peninsula were sinking as he passed, sinking and disappearing forever, so that even if he walked around the world he would only someday come to a final cape, with the empty sea beyond and the land he stood on sinking.

SIXTEEN

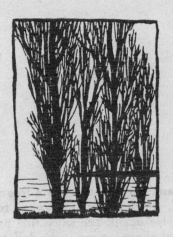

WALKING
EVERY DAY

As blank and bleached as a fragment of drift-wood, he sat and let waves break on his head. He drank the salty tide until he could drink no more, threw it up, crawled to the beach stream to drink. One afternoon it occurred to him that the currents could have shifted, she could have come ashore on the north beaches, or been swept by currents far down the peninsula to the west, past him. Those small white teeth chewing away at the rope — surely such pure will had lived! Surely the will to survive had something to do with survival!

Next morning he walked west on the spine, investigating every cove beach tucked out of the view of the crest trail. Days passed like that, he no longer remembered much of the night of the storm, it was too much like the memory of a dream, vague, incoherent, illuminated in flashes, intensely disturbing. We forget dreams, he thought, because they are too vivid to face. He sometimes had trouble remembering what had happened to him on the peninsula before the storm; once he couldn't recall what he was looking for, it was just something he did, climb up and down rocks step after step, looking closely at the margin of sea and shore, searching for patterns in the sand. Clouds rolled overhead, west to east in their own frilly groundswell, wave after wave of fronts, the masses of warm air wedging under the cold air and then rising like bubbles up through that drafty emptiness, clouds burgeoning into existence as the warm air expressed its watery milk.

For a week the sunsets were purest pink. Why in perfectly clear air some sunsets were pink, others bronze, others purple: he pondered that through many dusks, tending fires of driftwood started with a lens of clear glass he had found beachcombing. Through the long days he hiked westward and westward, roving from shore to shore. It was a task, a filling of the hours, a compulsion, a destiny. Kicking the rocks with the toe of his boot he heard chants come from his own mouth, wordless grunts, howls of pain, broken phrases: "And that. And that. And that. And that. And . . ."

Off to the right was a narrow ridge like a knife of rock, extending perpendicularly from the larger peninsula into the northern sea, disappearing over the horizon. It was so regular that it looked artificial, an impossibly long drawbridge connecting something over the horizon to the peninsula's great mass.

Where this ridge connected to the peninsula there stood the grass-covered walls of an old hill fort, which had perhaps served to defend this end of the drawbridge, who could say. Around the old grassy mounds were a cluster of driftwood crofts, their roofs made of sod. The people he found there were tiny, thin and brown. At their bidding he entered the largest croft and sat and ate with them, around the smoke of a peat fire. The east wall had two small windows, and shafts of sunlight shone motty through the reek.

Later he went back outside to escape the smoke. An old woman joined him and he saw that she cast no shadow except on her body. The sun was directly overhead, at least in this season, at midday. He thought about it for a while.

"Is there a trail over the ridge?" he asked the old woman.

"It is a trail narrow as virtue," she recited.

"What lies at the far end?"

"A temple, they say."

"How far away is it?"

She didn't know.

Driven by a bleached, dispassionate curiosity, he found the peninsular end of the ridge trail, and hiked out onto it. The trail was a ragged row of squarish marble stones, set in the edge of the splintered ridge. Sometimes it led over arches like littoral drawbridges, spanning blocky debris-choked seas.

He hiked in shifts, timing himself by the sun's slow flight, hoping to get some kind of regular "day's march" to measure the distance he traveled. The trail never got as narrow as the old woman had claimed it was. He hiked for ten days, then came to an enormous geometrical cone of dirt, overgrown with thick green grass and cut by the staircase that the trail here became. He hurried up these stone stairs and stepped onto a flagged circular terrace at the top, with the breath whooshing in his lungs and his blood pounding through him. Behind him the knife edge was a slender thread dropped over the sea, a kind of stone pier extending all the way to the watery horizon, which gave no clue of the peninsula. It was a frightening view.

But it was midday, so he took a straight stick from his pack and stuck it between two flagstones, so that it would cast its shadow to the north, over a square of yellow marble. A straight stick, straight up. Its shadow looked like the black dirt under a fingernail.

He sucked in his breath, measured the shadow with another stick he had brought, finely notched for the purpose. It was impossible to be very accurate with the shadow so miniscule, but he tried.

The stick was something like a thousand times longer than its shadow!

He sat down and thought it over, aware that this was not his idea, that somewhere in his blank past he had heard of the method, and admired it. But the details, the details. . . . A spasm of pain as he felt the presence of his lost past, a world in which one could stand on the accumulated knowledge of all those who came before, a world in which one could feel one knew something more than what blazed in the senses. . . . Think, think. If the shadow were the same length as the stick, then he would be halfway to the pole (discounting the curvature of the planet), and the world would be eight times his hike in circumference, or eighty marches around. Right? It seemed so.

But the shadow was only the thousandth part of the stick in length, and it had taken ten days to get here; so it would take ten thousand days to make it halfway to the pole, and therefore eighty thousand days to circumnavigate the globe. Was that right? Garth had once said that the years here were four hundred days long. So to walk around the world would take . . . two hundred years.

SEVENTEEN

THE PAST

On the way back to the peninsula it rained, and then even snowed a bit, a cold wet slushy snow, heavy flakes swirling down and filling the air with white clots. Clouds gusted onto him so that he could seldom see more than a few feet of the knife edge, and perhaps gray waves thrashing themselves to foam on rocks below. The wind keened over the ridge's obstruction, and he couldn't escape it without huddling below the ridge on the lee side, where the lack of movement made him just as cold as the wind would have. He had run out of the food the crofters had given him, and every night was a miserable eternity, so long he lost every hope. He could free himself to sleep through only a quarter or a third of those endless nights, and the dawns were a deep stabbing relief, not only physically but in his feelings.

Through the days in the snowy fog he hiked as long and hard as he could. There was a kind of moss that was a startling, unreal green, and it grew in a mixed pattern with a silvery gray bracken, and olive and yellow lichen; the colors made a quilt over the fresh white granite and distracted his eye as he walked, even to the point of making him unsteady. He began to sleep through midday and the early afternoon, and crawl along the path through much of the night, to generate warmth. He began to eat the moss.

One day, staggering along thinking about his days on the peninsula, he realized that even if his lost past before the night beach were suddenly to return to him, it would no longer matter in the slightest. Compared to what had happened to him since, any more distant past would seem no more than news of a previous incarnation—news of someone else.

That occurred to him in the late morning; and in the afternoon, after hours of tromping through slush and watching snowflakes swirl up the ridge and down the other side, it further occurred to him that if that were true, if the return of a forgotten past would mean nothing to his feelings, then it might also be true that the past's continuous and uninterrupted presence in his mind would not have made any difference in the situation. It might be that events more than a few months gone would always be nothing more than broken and fleeting images, images like those that fled from the mind each morning upon waking, fragments of dreams too powerful to face. The past was a dream.

EIGHTEEN

THE
QUEEN OF
DESIRE

Rising up over the horizon, the peninsula looked like the tall edge of a world-wrapping continent; there was no indication at all that the ocean stood just on the other side of that long wall of rock.

When he stood on the peninsula again, it felt like home, and he turned west with relief. On the southern slope it felt warm even under a steady blanket of cloud, so warm that he arched his shoulders and lay on rocks just to feel it. Then one day as he passed a small cove the sun broke out, and he ran down into the water, and rolled naked in the sand until a coat of it stuck everywhere to his skin, and he fell asleep on the beach baking in that layer of crushed rock and shell. He slept all day.

In the later afternoon he foraged for beach food, and that evening he walked easily along the southern slope, reveling in the warm air and his full belly. Just to be alive and thoughtless, an animal in its moment of pure duration, that was happiness enough. The flood of stars spilled across the sky, providing light enough to see the wide trail on the bluff above the southern beaches. Up and down over grassy hills he walked, until ahead of him he saw a cluster of lights, as if a constellation of yellow stars had fallen onto the spine.

Torches.

He approached carelessly because he was careless, and found himself in the outskirts of what once must have been a considerable town, sprawling over a plateau in the spine from north beach to south. Now many of the stone buildings were in ruins, big quartz blocks tumbled about the maze of streets, shattered in a way that suggested earthquake; many of the walls were only waist high. But in the center of town was a plaza flagged by turquoise and coral, smoothed to a sheen by centuries of wear, and around it several small buildings remained standing, lit by torches that flickered in the breeze atop short fat pillars.

Many people were gathered in this plaza, laughing and eating from long tables piled high with food: they greeted Thel cordially and without surprise, and bid him eat, watching his face and nudging each other with elbows. They wore feather capes over plain brown pants and skirts; various birds' most colorful plumage had been sewn together, so that there were capes of solid emerald or sapphire, others striped like metallic rainbows, yet others spotted with enormous eyes.

A tall black-haired woman wrapped in a full-length cape of ruby feathers emerged from the largest building, and approached Thel. She commanded the attention of all, and when she turned and gave instructions under her breath to a retinue of young women in blue, they hurried giggling back into the building.

The woman then smiled at Thel, and welcomed him in a commanding voice. "This is Olimbos, and I am Khora, its queen. Tonight we celebrate our new year, and the arrival of a stranger after sunset is a good sign. Will you join our celebration?"

Thel nodded and said he would.

The queen smiled, laughed; the citizens of Olimbos laughed with her, then chattered among themselves. Musicians playing hand drums and mandolins struck up a long flowing melody, which never seemed to end. More torches burned and the quartz blocks sparked all shot with light.

The queen sat at a table and ate. Some women gave Thel a plate of pungent cooked meat, and a tall glass of a fiery liquor that tasted of dune grass; it burned all the way to his stomach, and made his vision jump.

The young women serving the queen emerged with a long yellow cape, which they cast over Thel's shoulders as if throwing a net. Everyone cheered and the music picked up its tempo, the hand drums quick and insistent, the mandolins sweet and swaying. Thel had seen a small bird whose chest feathers were the color of his cape, a bird that flashed above streams as it struck the surface, a kind of kingfisher, its breast a glittering yellow in the shadows under the banks. It had taken a lot of them to make a cape so large. Thel drank more of the grass liquor and pulled the cape about him, pleased at its brightness. They gave him a chair to sit in, and he sat and watched.

When the tables of food were considerably emptier people stood and danced in the plaza, turning in groups of two, three and four, small steps punctuated by spins that swirled their capes in the air. The queen stood and walked among the dancers. She threw her cape back over her shoulders and Thel saw that she was naked under it. Her body was long and smoothly muscled, dramatic in the torchlight: as she walked among the dancers her hipbones jutted and swayed, flanking the long curve of her belly, which led the eye down to a tall mass of glossy black pubic hair. As Thel looked at this triangle of hair it bulged out and down like the tail of a panther, waving before the queen; then the cord of fur extended forward and grew into a cat's body and hind legs, which touched the ground as the forelegs and head bloomed out of the body's front end. A small black cat, yes, walking before the queen with its tail a sort of long leash, stretching back up and into the queen's pubic fur.

Thel swallowed heavily, and his pulse raced. He could not shift his gaze from the cat, and saw the queen's laughter only peripherally. She walked around the plaza toward him, and the black cat ranged from side to side ahead of her, its eyes two reflective dots of green torchlight. The dancers swirled in circles about the queen and Thel in his chair, shedding the clothes under their capes. Some kissed each other hungrily as they danced, others watched the queen approaching Thel.

She stood before him. The cat padded forward and rubbed itself against his ankles, purring loudly. The queen smiled. Her ribs moved with her quick breath. The small smile stayed on her lips, and her gaze wouldn't leave him.

The black cat jumped neatly into his lap, curled up there. The queen leaned forward, put her hands on his shoulders, kissed him. He felt the kiss, and then the blood pouring down into his penis, stiffening it under the cat's body.

The queen caught up his arms and pulled him to his feet, and he had to catch the cat in his hands. He could feel the little ribcage cradled in his palm, feel the vibration of its purr. The queen reached down and unfastened his pants, and they dropped around his ankles; as he stepped free each hard knock of his heart lifted his cock another notch, until it stood upright before his belly, feeling taut and live and full. Just to walk felt good with such an erection. The queen led him across the plaza to her residence, and dimly he heard the cheers of the dancers, mixed with the hand drums and mandolins.

Inside the building rugs and tapestries warmed one central room, which was lit by a score of small torches. A big square bed against one wall was piled high with quilted blankets, and the queen pulled Thel onto them, kissing him passionately. As they kissed the cat purred and licked at him, its little tongue rough against his skin. Thel thrust with his cock at the cat's head, and the long tail pulled back up into the queen until cat and cock disappeared in her, in one fluid purring motion. Then they were joined and the queen was laughing at his expression, rolling over onto him and riding his thrusts. She rolled sideways and Thel buried his face in her tangled hair and plunged away, and they rocked in rhythm to the hand drums for as long as he could hold on, until his spine shot great bolts of electric pleasure down and around and up, the pleasure radiating sideways in him until he felt it tingling in his arms, his hands, his face, all his skin.

Later as he lay beside her the black cat returned, purring and licking him back to life. The queen twisted so that she could lick at him along with the cat, and he was instantly stiff again. And so it went, through the night. Thel scarcely noticed the faces in the doorway to the chamber, and when he did, he didn't care.

In the blue just before sunrise he crawled past the guttering torches to his clothes and bags, left in the doorway by some thoughtful celebrant. The mirror was still in its bag, and on a whim he took it from its cloth sack and looked into it.

It was the queen's face — the male version of the queen's face, coarser and bearded, but recognizably hers. The queen stirred in her sleep on the bed, and he put the flat gold plate back in the bag. It fell heavily against his legs.

He returned to the bed, looked down at the sleeping queen. His head was cold. If only he could warm his ears; it seemed never once on this endless peninsula had he gotten his ears warm.

He got back under the blankets and snuggled next to her, put his ear against her ribs and heard her heart, beating quietly. She stirred and rolled toward him, pulled him to her; feeling her warmth triggered a wash of pure desire in him, and he melted again.

NINETEEN

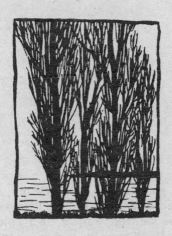

THE THEATER
OF GHOSTS

Days passed, and it stayed like that. Nothing seemed to warm him but Khora's touch. Otherwise he felt empty and cold. He swam under the sun, lay asleep on the beach, fished; and always cold.

Khora's people wandered the ruins of quartz, furtive by day and lascivious in the dusk, stroking each other, kissing, reaching inside each other's clothes. Nights were much darker and quieter than the festival night of Thel's arrival: the evenings punctuated by soft laughter and the gleam of one central torch, breaking its light in the big chipped blocks of quartz that lay around the plaza; and the long nights strange voyages of pleasure in the queen's big bedroom. The cat never again flowed out of her pubic mound, but the memory of it — the idea of it — inflamed Thel's imagination, at the same time that he was repulsed by it. In the bed she pushed him about, brought her maids in to watch, told him what to do, even slapped him hard in the face; and he began to find this more and more exciting, even though he hated her for it. He only seemed truly to live when he was in contact with her body. Everything changed then, the chamber seemed charged with color, and the stars in the doorway sparked as if engendered by a blow to the head.

Then one night—he had lost track of time, it seemed he had been in this life for weeks and weeks—the routine changed, and they lit four torches and set them at the corners of the plaza, and sat at the center among their crossed shadows. The queen walked among them, naked under her long red cape.

"You wonder how this world came to be," she said to Thel.

He shrugged, surprised. In fact he had stopped wondering long before. He didn't know what to say.

The queen laughed at his expression. "You talk in your sleep, you see. Now listen. Everything is full of gods. And in the beginning the sea god filled the universe. The sea's ideas were bubbles, and one bubble idea she called love, and all the water in the universe fell into that bubble, taking all the other gods with it. Most drowned, but two learned to swim, and these were the gods rock and dragon. These two loved the sea goddess, and for ages they swam in her and the three were lovers, and all was well until dragon went away, and came back and found rock plunged to ocean's very center, an embrace dragon could never know, for rock did not need to breathe, and dragon did. And in a rage dragon flew away and grew as big as the sky, and reached back with one bony hand and clenched it around the two lovers, cutting through ocean's body to grasp rock and strangle him. And rock died; and the sea goddess, cut in half, died; and seeing his two lovers dead, dragon died. And the bubble burst, leaving nothing but a theater of ghosts. And the lovers' bodies rotted, until nothing of dragon was left but his skeleton; nothing of rock but his heart; nothing of ocean but her salty blood. And ages later dragon's skeleton broke away and flew off through the empty sky, scattering its bones that are the stars. Only the bones of the hand which had strangled the lovers remained there, wrapping the round drop of ocean's blood, cutting it down to rock. All who live on the remains of these three are accidental vermin, walking an edge of bone, which is highest at the old wristbones, and nearly submerged where forefinger once met thumb. We live by drinking ocean, eating rock, and standing on the dragon's bones."

And Khora laughed bitterly, and walked toward Thel with a stalking, vengeful lust.

TWENTY

THE CRUCIBLE
OF SOULS

Cold days on the beach, warm nights in the queen's bed. In the evenings sometimes she stripped him bare, aroused him and then led him out among her subjects, tugging on his erection as if it were a leash. He would flush with shame and an intense arousal, and back on her bed he felt his orgasms as if a too-large spine were erupting out of him; his life; she would take one more portion of it from him, laughing and gasping, her long supple torso contracting across the stomach while she came herself.

It was horrible, and each time he hoped it would last forever. During the days he could hardly wait for the next night, and he spent some part of each afternoon lying on the sand, dreaming of the moment when he would be led through the crowd, tugged this way and that by his imperious queen.

When one of her people told her that he owned the mirror, she laughed and made him show his reflection to the night's gathering. Her face, her masculine face, stared out of the smooth gold surface, surrounded by a halo of torchlight, and when Thel rubbed his hand over his jaw trying to feel if there were an actual correspondence with the image, the villagers howled.

Afterward the queen showed no more interest in the mirror. This was a relief to him, because now it seemed that the mirror was his only friend, and sometimes he would take the bag on walks down the beach and let the mirror out and set it flat on the sand, the wet round gold surface indigo with reflected sky, and turning it every way but at himself and his traitor's face, he saw in it the beach he had been born on, the cliffs he had first climbed to get up on the crest, the spine king's bloody camp, the horse meadows, all a past that felt as remote to him as a life among the stars. Grains of sand on a circle of golden indigo, the limpid sky marred by a small fluttering dot, a kestrel hanging on the wind. . . .

When he looked up and saw the little hawk was real, he rolled off his belly surprised, and sat up to watch it. It stood feathering on its column of air, falcon's beak pointed down at the sea as it darted down and held itself back, darted and held back, then sideslipped and carved the wind with a splay of strong wings, before settling again in the invisible current. A windhover.

TWENTY-ONE

A FACE

He trod home through soft sand, the image of the hawk fixed in his mind. That night Khora's dominion seemed more sad and degraded than ever, a tired performance of a play whose audience had long since gone away, the mating automatic, the torch gleam on the quartz a tawdry effect of colored light, nothing more. And yet he behaved just as always.

Stirring in the queen's disordered bed, then driven out into the silent night by his thoughts, Thel stared up at the stars, feeling himself draining out of his body with his wine-scented piss. The torchlight snagged in the cracks in the quartz, and he stood for long moments, mindless.

By the ruddy light he saw a face rise over a broken wall. He stepped toward it and she stood up from behind the wall—the swimmer, gesturing for silence.

He fell running to her, but when he stood she was still there, hopping the wall to come to him, finger crossing lips as she whispered "Shh, shh, shh," and he was holding her, holding that strong hard body and then he pushed her back to look at her. Still her: it made him weep and laugh at once in the same hot convulsion of his face, it was her, no doubt of it, standing right before him as real as his living hand. "I thought you were dead," he whispered.

"And I you." Her voice. "Come on, get your things. Clothes, sandals, some food."

"They'll stop us."

She looked around. "They're asleep. Drunk sleep."

Irrational fear spiked through him. "She'll stop us." And explained: "Their queen, she has . . . powers."

"Don't wake her, then. Be quick about it, and quiet."

So he tiptoed back into the queen's chamber, over the crumpled tapestries and her snoring courtiers, and picked up pants and boots and the mirror in its bag, averting his head so that he would not see Khora's sleeping face, never see it again, and the pain of that was completely flooded in a rising elation, he skipped out the broad arched doorway into the plaza where a false dawn streaked the eastern horizon and made the guttering torchlight pale and ghastly. There the swimmer took his hand and led him out of the ruins west and up a tumbled boulderslope to the crest of the spine, where they could see the light pool of the sea split by the dark peninsula, and the sky darkly luminous and semi-transparent, revealing for an instant the world behind the sky, and he could always have done this, could always have just walked on westward, but the swimmer had shown him the way; still astounded by her presence he started to run, pulled her along in her clumsy swimmer's gait and they ran along the spine trail.

TWENTY-TWO

EXFOLIATION

It was like being born again. They hiked through the long days napping only briefly at midday, and wandered the long dusks hunting for food on the beaches, swimming and then sleeping in sand. In the midnights Thel rose and walked about looking at stars till he chilled, then returned to the swimmer and her blanket.

One night when he returned to the swimmer, lying against her back with an arm over her and feeling her bottom shift back into his belly, he noticed the wind pouring over them. They were sleeping on the very edge of a beach cliff, just for the fun of the views at sunset and dawn, tucked into a hollow scooped at the cliff's edge, and wind was tearing down and out to sea; but as he had walked around the central plateau of the peninsula the night had been perfectly still, he had noticed it particularly. He got up and walked back out onto the hills, and again it was still; and at the cliff's edge, windy. He roused the swimmer and moved them inland a bit for the second half of the night. "The weight of the air keeps me awake," he told her. "It's falling over the edge."

He found out what had happened to her in the time since the storm on the brough, but only in snatches, in response to his questions. She had bitten her way free of the rope, as he had guessed. She had swum for a long time, she couldn't say how long, but from the way she spoke of it (or didn't), he thought it might have been very long indeed; days, certainly. She had landed on the southern side, and, assuming they had all survived and made it to the cape, she had walked back to it and searched for them, but found nothing. She waited there for a long time, regaining her strength and assuming she would see Birsay, escorting other travelers across; but no one ever appeared, and so finally she started west again. Groups traveling east to west passed her, and she had hidden from them, afraid that they might be the spine kings or the sorcerers. And then one night she had come on him in the ruins.

"We may have been wandering on the opposite sides of that cape at around the same time," Thel said. "And even along the peninsula." It was painful to think that he could have avoided the whole episode at Khora's, simply by making an arbitrary change of direction that would have resulted in running into the swimmer earlier. "Ah, but then I spent a long time out on the drawbridge, as I called it. Did you see that?" He described it; she had, but had passed by it without stopping.

"We're lucky we ever met again at all," she said. "It's a big world."

"But narrow." The thought of never meeting her again made him shiver. "As long as we both continued westward. . . ."

"We were lucky. We've always been lucky."

One night after lying down and talking for a while they rolled together and kissed, then mated, and at first he was frightened, but it was such an affirmation, such a gesture of liking, that it was hard for him to believe it was the same act he had performed with Khora. It wasn't, really, and the difference was such that he began to find it hard to remember those nights in the queen's chamber; they slipped away, except in certain dreams that woke him trembling.

As they continued westward the peninsula rose in elevation again, the backbone of pure granite breaking up out of the sea and sand and climbing like the edge of some enormous battered scimitar. They walked without urgency, merely to walk, to create a good space between themselves and Khora and all that lay behind, and each day was spent watching where each step went, climbing the shattered staircase of stone, becoming intimate with the local granite, an ever-modulating mixture of feldspars pink or orange or yellow, big clear grains of quartz, flecks of black hornblende. These three types of rock, jumbled and melded, forming the hard cracked fin of granite lifting out of the sea: it was hard for Thel not to be mesmerized by such a thing, to imagine it amelt and flowing like candle wax under the immense pressures inside the earth.

They came to a long straight stretch of the spine, where the feldspar was white and the hornblende just freckled the mix, making it the whitest granite possible. Here the southern side of the spine became a perfectly vertical drop to the sea, while the northern flank offered a gentle rocky slope to a wide white beach. The trail stayed well away from the southern cliff, but at midday or dusk they sometimes walked up to the edge to take a look down, and one evening in a dulcet sunset they looked over the edge and found that the whole cliff was a single gigantic overhang, as if the spine had been tipped to the south. They looked straight down at the sea, and could see nothing of the upper third of the cliff under them.

Quickly they stepped back, then lay flat and crawled forward, to stick their heads over the edge and have another look. The two or three thousand feet of the cliff looked like the curved inner wall of a shallow cave; they lay on an immense overhang. Thel could feel his stomach trying to reach through his skin and clamp onto the rock, like an abalone muscle; the drop was such that he and the swimmer laughed, in an instinctive attempt to ward off the fear of it. Thel crawled back and grabbed a loose rock that was as heavy as he cared to play with in that area, and shoved it over the edge. They watched it fall until it was a speck that disappeared, but the splash was bigger, a brief burst of white in the flat plate of blue, a *long* distance offshore from the cliff's bottom. They exclaimed at the sight, and did it again, and then they lay there until the light was almost gone, hypnotized by the lascivious false sense of danger, the sublimity. Mid-dusk a flock of seabirds rose up from the water in spiraling gyres, big white birds like cormorants that apparently nested in cracks or arches in the exfoliated cliff under them, out of their sight—for the birds rose and rose, tilting together on updrafts, flapping and banking, growing bigger, shifting this way and that like bubbles rising in water.

TWENTY-THREE

NAUTILUS
UNIVERSE

A week or so later the spine twisted south and dropped again, fanning out into a big broken rockfield, granite hills and knobs faulted with long grabens that had become skinny ponds or rectangular pools, or thin meadows that cut the rock from beach to beach. Up and down they walked over this terrain, sometimes on the trail which continued to snake its way along the path of least action, or else rambling over the rock, down into a meadow, up ledges, over the rock, down into another grassy swale. It was good land, dotted with trees that clung to the steep jumbles of rock and soil that walled the meadows: foxtail pines, no taller than the two travelers but with thick riven trunks, and bare dead branches spiking out of them in every direction. Steep bluffs stood over the white bay beaches, and many of the bluff tops were rimmed by a tuck of these foxtails, growing crabbed and horizontal in the winds.

They crossed this land for many days, and one

afternoon when they were foraging on the southern beach for food, they came upon a shallow bay, a perfect arc of a circle. The bluffs backing the bay were cut by sandy ravines, and between bluff and beach there was a crescent of dunes covered with olive and silver grass.

Scattered over the dunes in irregular rows were sea shells as big as houses. They resembled nautilus shells in which the smaller segments have been pulled a bit out to the side, but they stood about three or four times Thel's height. Their thick curved walls were colored in complex spiraling patterns of brown or deep purple trapezoids, which turned with the shape of the shells and grew smaller and smaller as they twisted around to an invisible center point, like the eyefaces of the facewomen.

Thel and the swimmer walked among these specimens in awe, observing how they gleamed in the late afternoon light, for each one appeared to have been polished as smooth as glass; and there were even, they saw, windows of some clear material replacing some of the brown and purple trapezoids, high in the curved sides.

They were just looking under the bottom edge of one shell when a short brown woman ducked out and regarded them suspiciously. "Who are you?" she demanded, touching the thick edge of her shell, looking as though she might bolt back under at any second. "What are you doing?"

"I am a swimmer," the swimmer said gently. "This is Thel. We are travelers from east of the brough. We seek nothing of you, and will leave if our presence makes you unhappy."

"No, no," the woman said. "Not necessary." As she spoke, others ducked out from their shell cottages, people small like the woman, and with leathery skin of brown or purplish cast. They were a nervous crowd,

and as they shuffled about the two they moved away re-
flexively each time the swimmer gestured. But in the
end they welcomed the two cordially enough, and invited them to eat with them, a varied meal of fish and
seaweed bits, washed down by a sparkling liquor that
made the two instantly drunk. The shell people offered
them a shell of their own to spend the night in, and they
agreed, dropping to hands and knees to get under the
edge of one really large brown-flecked specimen.

Once inside it much resembled other beach cottages, or so the swimmer said. Cut plank floors had
been set flat in each chamber, with plank staircases
leading through holes cut from one chamber to the
next. In each chamber driftwood furniture was covered with padded cloth made of fine seaweed hair, on
which simple striped patterns had been printed with
shell dyes. There were knickknacks from the sea on
the curved walls, and in an upper chamber a small bed
was tucked under a window, across from a brick fireplace cut into the central wall. Each chamber had a
window cut in its outer wall, the trapezoids filled with
a clear fibrous material in the lower chambers where
the windows were big, with mosaics of colored
driftglass upstairs where the windows were small.

The swimmer observed it all with a delighted, little girl's smile, unlike any Thel had seen on her face.
"It's just like my aunt and uncle's," she kept saying. "I
used to love visiting them."

So they spent the night dry and warm, cuddled
together in a narrow bed, and in the morning the shell
people were out working the beach or the ravines or
the meadows up above the bluffs. Their next-door
neighbor said to them, "If you will collect puka shells
for us, you can stay in that house for as long as you
care to. It hasn't been used in ages."

Collecting puka shells, they found, was a simple
business, so simple that the shell people found it tedi-

ous; all of them but the children had more interesting or important things to do. Nevertheless they loved having the jewelry made from these shells. On the steep strand of the bay a vicious shorebreak sluiced the coarse blond sand back and forth, and as it did it ground up all the shells and coral bits and rocks that had found their way there, turning them into more of the coarse sand. Their next-door neighbor showed the two travelers that among the shell fragments being washed up and down were many specimens of a small fat cone-shaped shell, all of which were being worn down until only the thick caps at the base of the cone remained, round and usually holed in the middle, at the centerpoint of the shell's whorl where it had been quite thin to begin with. So at a certain point in their disintegration these round flat holed pieces made perfect necklace beads, ready to be strung and worn; and a tiny percentage of them were a rich, deep blue, the color of the sky in mid-twilight. These blue pieces the shell folk treasured, and the most important members of the community wore many necklaces and bracelets and anklets of the blue buttons, and every shell person owned at least one big necklace of them.

The easiest method of finding them was simple, they were told. Stand in the shorebreak facing the shore, and as the waves sluiced back down over the coarse sand, one saw thousands of fragments of pastel shell color. Once every dozen or score of waves one saw a flash of the blue, a flash that somehow suggested it was not a jagged tiny fragment but a complete cap; and then with a quick pounce and some luck one could snatch it up, in a streaming handful of wet sand.

So Thel and the swimmer spent a day hunting puka shells, and at sunset they each had a small belt bag filled with the little blue circles. The shell folk were tremendously pleased, and fed them a feast of squid, shark, seaweed salad, and corn. And the day had passed pleasantly enough, and the swimmer remained delighted with their curved shell home; and so they decided to stay a while.

Soon enough they found that all was not peaceful among the shell folk. In fact they were all involved in ceaseless conflicts with one another, and alliances and social wars among them were quick, constant and volatile. The division among them between brown skin and purple seemed part of the conflict, but in some original sense that had been long since lost in subsequent permutations; now purple-skinned folk were likely to refer to themselves as brown, and vice versa, and they all wore clothing and shell jewelry in color codes, to indicate where their loyalties stood on any given day. The important shifts in alliances and enemies were marked by the physical moving of their shell homes. The inhabitants, never more than one or two to a shell, would enlist friends and drag their home over the sand to a new neighborhood, sent on their way by bursts of violent cursing from their old neighbors, and leaving a swath through the sand to mark the dramatic event. The bay beach was crisscrossed by these trails, which wind and tide erased quickly enough; but there were always new tracks to replace the old. Psara, a lithe graceful man with purple skin that was the darkest in the village, explained to them that this was a fundamental part of their nature, and with a broad white smile he offered an explanation: "There are too few of us to reproduce properly if there is anything short of a total mixture. We cannot afford tribes or even families of any extent. Besides"— he grinned— "we are descended from crabs, and inclined to be solitary and feisty. An argument a day and you live forever, we say."

Thel and the swimmer found this a bit much, and one day they decided to take advantage of the mobility of residence, and they got Psara and some others to help them drag their shell out to the edge of the village, just inside the broad eastern point of the bay, beside a stream, behind a dune, and all by themselves. Their old neighbors shouted abuse at them as they left, but in a friendly tone, and they dropped by later to help return all the furniture to its proper place, and to trade for the previous day's catch of puka shells.

TWENTY-FOUR

PURE
DURATION

And so they fell into the rhythm of the bay, into their own rhythm. They had their home, isolated from the battles and out under the eastern point's bluff. That whole stretch of beach they had to themselves, especially in the mornings; and the point was washed by the tides, and was an especially rich source of the blue shells.

Each strangely long day became a sort of eternity in itself. In the mornings the air was cool and clear and salty, the sea calm and the sun blazing over it. They stood calf-deep in the tumbling waves, facing the beach and the granite bluff behind, watching the water and sand mix wildly in the water, tiny shell fragments of pink and brown and yellow and purple and red tumbling over each other among the clear and white and tan grains of sand, all a tumble and a rush of wet brilliant color with the clear foam-flecked water pouring over it, and once in a while a flash of blue like a dark sky would reveal itself among the rest and they

would dive, scoop up handfuls of sand, let it sift
through fingers until the blue fragment was there to
be plucked out and put in a bag. If they proved to
have missed it, they groaned and started again. And it
seemed it would be morning forever.

At midday they sat on the beach and ate something, and slept on the sand or talked, and it seemed
the midday would last forever, a warm lazy eternal
nap; and then in the afternoons they would walk the
beach in search of food or the rare overlooked blue
button poking out of the dry sand, or get in the surf
and hunt again, and it seemed the afternoon would
never end, the sun white and stationary in the broad
western sky. Only at sunset did it seem time passed:
slow, stately, the sun dropped and slowed as it
dropped, it seemed, until it stood on the horizon
chopped into orange slices by the layering of the atmosphere, and they had time to climb the bluffs and
watch the mallow sea go indigo and the air become
visible and the pared sun turn to a yellow sliver, then
an emerald green dot, the green flash that ended the
sunset. And then they were in the endless dusk, all its
dark grainy colors filling with blackness as the eternal
night came on. And this was just one day in an eternal
round of unchanging days, until Thel felt that they
lived forever every couple of weeks; and beyond that,
in the unimaginable fullness of whole years, lay the
touch of pure duration.

TWENTY-FIVE

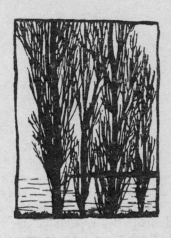

CASTAWAY

Most of these endless days they spent alone, but sometimes one or more of the shell folk would drop by, especially the children, who were delighted to see them do something as childish as recover pukas. Their most frequent adult companion was Psara, who occasionally joined them in the surf, laughing at the sport but incredibly fluid and quick-eyed and quick-handed at it; he could collect more blue shells in a morning than Thel could in a couple of days. As he dove and spluttered in the shorebreak he regaled them with the village gossip, which was consistently lurid and melodramatic, a never-ending extravaganza of petty feuds and sordid sexual affairs. He also invited them in to the rare festival nights, when everyone came out to a driftwood fire by the biggest stream and drank the clear liquor until they were all maudlin with drunken affection for one another, their feuds forgotten in the brilliant yellow light of festival reality. They would dance in rings around the fire, holding hands and crashing left and right, embracing their partners, and declaring them wonderful browns or purples.

During one of these parties, late, when the fire was a pile of pulsing embers and the shell folk were comatose with liquor and neighborly feeling, Psara regarded the two beachcombers with his quick ironic smile, and slipped over to them and put a sensuous hand on the swimmer's broad shoulder, and on Thel's. "Would you like to hear a story?"

The two nodded easily.

"Paros," Psara said loudly, and the oldest person there jerked upright, peered around sleepily. "Tell us the story of the castaways, Paros!" and several children said, "Yes, please, please!"

Old Paros nodded and stood precariously. "This is a story from the world's beginning, when ocean never equaled gleamed in the dark, perfect and white and empty. Across her white body sailed a raft, not our ship of fools but an orderly and good society, the brown and the purple having little to do with each other but coexisting in peace." Some of the villagers laughed at that.

"But one day a brown man and a purple woman met at the mast, and talked, and later they did it again, and again, and when the browns and the purples bathed over the side they dove under the raft and swam together for a time; and they fell in love.

"Now both of them were married, and their partners were prominent in the societies of brown and purple. So when the two were finally discovered, all the browns and purples were outraged, and there were calls to drown the two lovers.

"But the raft sailed by an island in the white sea, the smallest speck of land—a rock, a tree, a shell and a stream. And the browns and purples decided to maroon the two lovers, and threw them overboard, and the two swam to the island. And as they swam, ocean never equaled seeped into their minds and took all memory of the raft away from them, so that they would not despair.

"And they landed on the island, and the raft sailed away and would never come back. The woman gave birth to many children, and the children quarreled and would have killed each other. So ocean never equaled made the island longer, so that there would be room for the children and grandchildren of the two lovers to live without mortal strife between them. But they fought and multiplied at such a rate that ocean never equaled had to stretch the island all the way around her, to give them room to chase each other endlessly; and the white sea turned blue with the blood and tears shed."

Silence. Paros sat down. Gray film fluttered on the dull coals of the fire. Thel felt as though he were falling, he had to clasp the swimmer's arm to steady himself, even though they were sitting.

Later as they walked back home he stumbled once or twice, though he had not drunk that much. And several times he started to speak, and stopped; and he noticed the swimmer did the same. And that night in their narrow bed they hugged each other like two frightened children, lost at night in the woods.

TWENTY-SIX

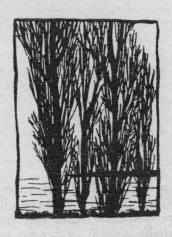

WE ARE
CLOUDS

Days passed. In the summer the shallows got so hot that they had to swim offshore to get any refreshment from the sea, and they searched for shells naked, as brown as the brown shellfolk. In the winter the water was so cold that it hurt their ankles as it rushed over their feet, and each day their skin turned as purple as the purple shellfolk, teeth chattering so that the fire in their bedroom was a lovely warmth. They spent storm days sitting in the bed watching the fire and talking and making love, while wind and rain lashed at their streaming window. Days like that were wonderful to Thel, but better yet were the long summer days, knee deep in surf under the sun, the intense rays pulsing on his neck in what felt like discrete little pushes of light and heat. He would look up from the sand tumbling in the white-water and see the swimmer make some graceful move, her naked brown body twisting as she dove for a blue fragment, or streaming with water as she stood up af-

ter a dive; or the muscles of her arms rippling like
backwash hitting an oncoming wave; or the sight of
her legs and bottom and back as she walked away
down the beach; or the tilt of her head as she walked
toward him, looking down at the whitewater; and his
heart would swell like an erection inside him and he
would run through the broken surf and tackle her,
kissing her neck and face until she laughed at him and
they would make love there, with water and sand running over them. And sometimes she would run up and
tackle him and they would do the same. And after-
wards they would play grunion in the surf, lying in the
shorebreak and rolling up and down with the broken
waves, taking the sea in and spurting it out like foun-
tains, not thinking a thing. Every part of the day eternal, on summer days like that.

But the sun moved, and time passed nevertheless.
Sitting in the shorebreak and watching his lover roll
back and forth like beautifully rounded driftwood,
Thel couldn't help thinking of that, from time to time;
of time passing: and he wished he could be a man of
bronze, unchanging, living the same day over and
over. He would have chosen that day.

Looking across the bay, he saw clouds rushing
over the granite boulders of the point. Both granite
and cloud had deeply complex textured surfaces, but it
was startling to think how different they were in their
mutability. Each moment the clouds changed and
would never be the same; while the point rocks would
remain much as they were now, ages after he and the
swimmer were forever gone. Reflecting on this he was
surprised when she rolled into him on a wave and
said, "We are clouds." And even more surprised when
he heard himself reply, "But mountains are clouds,
too."

TWENTY-SEVEN

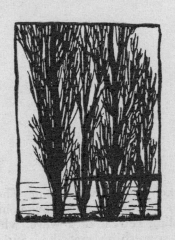

AN
OLD COIN

Another day, in late autumn, Thel was standing in the surf, hunting pukas in the colorful tumbling retreat of a wave, when he saw a bright flash—something metallic—and his pounce, trained now to a fine accuracy, brought it up in his sand-streaming hands: an old coin, worn almost smooth but still bright, a color between the gold of the mirror's surface and the bronze of a bronze sunset. One side held the profile of a head, and holding it up to see it better, Thel caught sight of his swimmer with her close-cropped head in profile some yards away; and it was exactly her profile on the coin. The same strong nose, full mouth, distinct jaw, high forehead: as exact an image as a black paper silhouette cut by a sidewalk artist, in some life he could not otherwise remember. It had to be her. And yet the coin was obviously ancient, the remnant of a long dead civilization.

Thel pocketed the coin, and that night in their

shell cottage he put it on the brick mantel of their chimney, next to the spot where light occasionally pulsed through the wall, from the mirror hung in the next chamber. He said to the swimmer, "Were you ever the queen of an ancient kingdom?"

"Yes," she muttered sleepily. "And I still am."

But this, he supposed, was another of their misunderstandings. Thel had first noticed this phenomenon when he had seen a windhover, hunting over the meadows inland. "Look," he had said, "a kestrel." But the swimmer had thought him crazy for pointing into the sky, for that to her was the name of a kind of fish. And later he found that when he said *loyalty* he understood it to mean *stubbornness*, and when she said *arbitrary* she meant *beautiful*, and that when she said *melancholy* she did not mean that sadness we enjoy feeling, but rather *mendacity*; and when she said *actually* she meant *currently*; and when he said "I love you," she thought he was saying "I will leave you." They had slowly worked up quite a list of these false cognates, Thel could recite scores and scores of them, and he had come to understand that they did not share a language so much as the illusion of a language; they spoke strong idiolects, and lived in worlds of meaning distinct and isolated from the other. So that she no doubt understood *queen of an ancient kingdom* to mean something like *a swimmer in the deep sea*; and the mystery of the ancient alloy coin was never explained, and, he realized, never would be. It gave him a shiver of fear, thinking about it—it seemed to him that nothing would ever be explained, and that all of a sudden each day was slipping away, that time was flying by and they were getting old and nothing would ever come clear. He sat on the beach watching the clouds tumble overhead and letting handfuls of sand run through his fingers, the little clear grains of quartz, flecks of black mica, pieces of coral, shell fragments

like small bits of hard ceramic, and he saw that a sub-
stantial portion of the sand was made of shells, that
living things had labored all their lives to create ceramic shelters, homes, the most permanent parts of
themselves; which had then been pummeled into
shards just big enough to see, millions upon millions of
lives ground up and strewn under him, the beach
made out of the wreckage of generations. And before
long he and the swimmer too would become no more
than sand on a beach; and they would never really
have understood anything.

TWENTY-EIGHT

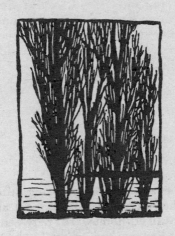

FESTIVAL

One evening in early spring, after a long day on the hot tawny beach, Thel and the swimmer walked homeward, between great logs of driftwood that had washed ashore in the winter. In the blue twilight the logs looked like the bodies of fallen giants after a titanic battle, and above them in the sky a black star was fluttering, a bird high in the air. The swimmer clasped Thel's arm: "Look," she said, and pointed down the beach. "We have visitors." Torchlight glimmered around their shell home, a dozen points of yellow weaving in the dusk.

It was a group of the shellfolk, drinking liquor from curved shells and laughing as they danced in a circle around their home.

"Is it New Year's already?" the swimmer asked.

"Something else," Thel said.

They walked into the circle of light, and the shellfolk greeted them and explained it was Paros's birthday, and, as had happened once or twice before,

they had decided to celebrate out at Thel and the
swimmer's home, because they had not been able to
agree whether brown or purple should host. So Thel
and the swimmer joined the party, and ate and danced
around the bonfire, and drank the liquor until everything was bright with the colors of fire and night, and
the faces of the shellfolk were like crude masks of
their daytime selves. Thel stumbled as he swung his
feet out in dance, and a face the brown nearest black
appeared before him, harsh with laughter and some
shouted curse he didn't understand. Then someone the
purple nearest black darted from the side, trying to
trip him; Thel looked up and it seemed that people
were not quite themselves, so that when Psara came
out of their house holding the mirror overhead, Thel
saw immediately that it was not Psara but Tinou.
Tinou's black skin was now purplish in tint, and his
face was twisted into Psara's visage, but with Tinou's
big grin on it, and Tinou's shouting laugh.

As the transformed shellfolk seized Thel and the
swimmer by the arms and dragged them to Tinou, a
part of Thel was distracted, wondering if Psara had
been Tinou all along, waiting all these years for whatever unimaginable reason to reveal himself—or if he
had recently arrived in the village, and for reasons
equally beyond comprehension had taken over Psara's
form. In any case the voice was the same, and as
Tinou placed the mirror in the wooden frame familiar
from Oia, he laughed and said, "All life is a case of
déjà vu, don't you think? And here we are again. Let
us put the woman through first, so Thel can see what
it looks like."

Thel struggled against the hands holding him
down, but there were too many of them; all his neighbors, faces gleaming yellow and their eyes big and
hungry as they watched the other group lift the strug-
gling swimmer and force her feet into the bright liquid

surface of the mirror. Tinou laughed and began his lit-
any of questions, face inches from hers, spittle flying
over her as he shouted in a gross parody of solicitous-
ness, "Pinching? pressing? gnawing? cramping?
crushing? wrenching? scalding? searing?" Thel was
proud of her, the way she could hold her face rigid in
a mask of stoic disgust, staring Tinou in the eye; but
his stomach was flip-flopping inside him as he saw the
flesh of her legs and torso jerk at the contact with the
mirror. Her body remained visible on the other side,
flesh pale and inert yet still there among them. But remembering his own voyage on the other side, Thel
feared they would be separated again, separated for
good, and as her head popped through and she tumbled unconscious to the ground behind the mirror,
Thel ripped convulsively away from the hands holding
him and leaped forward to dive head first through the
mirror and after her. The last thing he saw was Tinou's
face, bright with torchlight and astonishment, as big
around as the mirror itself.

TWENTY-NINE

THE
PURSUIT

It was early morning, sun bright in his eyes. The swimmer lay next to him, sleeping or unconscious, and the world smelled as fresh as the shadows under trees. It hurt to move—to raise his head, to sit up—each joint a stab of pain when he moved it. Nevertheless he was happy to be with her still.

And yet it hurt, it hurt to move. This was an aspect of pain he noticed at once: it was hard to see through it to anything else. It took a discipline that would have to be learned.

Groaning, he rolled to her side and shook her awake. She woke with a gasp and held her left arm to her side. They sat up, looked around at a cold windy hillside—the spine, in fact, near the crest, on a prominence overlooking the sea. There was no sign of the shellfolk's bay. "The sun," the swimmer said. "It's moving east. It will set in the east."

Thel ignored the conundrum of how she could

orient herself by something other than the sun in the sky, and merely nodded. "It's the mirror world," he said. "Everything's backwards."

They would need clothes, having been thrust into this world nearly naked. Even something like the leaf capes that the treefolk had worn would help shelter them from the wind.

Then the swimmer pointed. "Look, it's him. The thing that took over our Psara." Far to the east, on the crest of the spine, a figure was walking away from them. It had a lump on its back. "He's carrying the mirror," the swimmer said. She had a hand shading her eyes, and was squinting. "It's Tinou, isn't it."

"Yes." Thel peered after the tiny figure speculatively. "If we could get the mirror from him, and push through it again. . . ."

It might end the pain. It might return them to their hot tawny beach. It might. . . . They looked each other in the eyes, stood with some difficulty, followed the figure east.

It was hard going, even on the trail. At sunset each day they descended to the beach, the sun sinking into the eastern sea. Over time they wove capes of palm and fan seaweed; and each night they foraged for food, and the swimmer found a mollusk that when eaten dulled the pain of her arm, and Thel's joints. But the spine was getting higher and higher as they moved farther to the mirror east, and the trail stayed right on the crest of the spine, and the descent to the beaches became more difficult. Tinou stayed about the same distance ahead of them, so perhaps he was descending to water each night as well; but finally one sunset it was impossible, and the next, possible but too strenuous to contemplate. Besides, in the dusk the swimmer caught sight of Tinou, sitting next to the trail far above them; so they slept tucked in a fault to get out of the wind, and it was cold but they found birds' nests, and were able to raid them for food. Holes and dips in the granite held rainwater for their thirst, and the swimmer had dried a collection of the mollusks for their pain. But they ran out quickly enough.

Because the spine continued to rise they caught sight of Tinou several times a day, always most of a day's walk ahead of them, a speck against the pinkish broken granite of the spine's bony edge. The peninsula here resembled the precipitous blade of rock that Thel had traversed with the treefolk, a knife edge of scarcely weathered granite slicing the world ocean into two halves, so many thousands of feet high that the waves were no more than the faintest pattern of curves on the sea; and yet if the peninsula had been nothing but dunes, it would have been only a morning's walk to cross it from sea to sea. Higher and higher this great ridge arched into the sky, in irregular swoops, with many small ridge peaks, and an unhappily large number of sudden drops in the ridge line that they were forced to climb down, and then up again. As they made their way they sometimes saw broken bird nests scattered down the cliffs to right and left, the precious meat of eggs burst and dried over the rocks and sticks: Tinou had been kicking them apart as he passed, and so must have known they were following.

When the swimmer's mollusks were gone, they hiked on in pain; her arm never healed, and Thel's joints creaked as if filled with grit, and each day's march added to their scrapes, bruises, sprains: and none of these ever seemed to heal. In the mirror world their bodies had lost that ability. Hunger plagued them as well, but not thirst; some of the ponds they passed had Tinou's feces floating in them, but there were more of the little granite pools than he could find to foul, and they drank as deeply as if they might be able to get their sustenance from water alone. They ate mice, and birds, and eggs, and once a whole glorious patch of blueberries; then later, the bright green moss that Thel had found on the drawbridge. There was a lot of this moss as they climbed higher—moss, and blotchy lichen, and junipers and foxtail pines that up here were nothing but little wind-tortured bushes, tucked between boulders and down in cracks. They slept under these piney shrubs, and tried eating their cones but couldn't.

One evening in the indigo twilight Thel looked at the swimmer's bright pain-filled eyes. It was hard to remember the world on the other side of the mirror, their life on the hot tawny beach—a blur, a moment like the snapping of fingers, a dream. He said, "We never gain on him, and we're going slower every day. My joints—" he stopped, wanting to cry. "I'm hungry," he said instead.

She gave him a handful of the moss. He noticed that her fingers were narrower and longer, with full webs of skin between them, and a dusting of blond fur over the backs of the hands. She said, "Whatever happens, you must accept it."

He ate, considering what that implied. His own hands were gnarled and his thumbs were longer and less opposed to the fingers than they used to be. Flickering, pulsing, throbbing, shooting, lancing, cutting, rasping, splitting, yes. All of these. "Maybe," he said, feeling his face and the enlarged jaw, "maybe if we made an extraordinary effort. If we hiked all night—if we kept hiking till we caught him, you know. He's sleeping at night like we are, or we'd never be keeping pace with him. If we dispensed with that, and hiked all night. . . ."

"Tomorrow," she said, sleepy. Her nose was smaller, and it twitched at the end. "One last night of rest, and we'll start tomorrow."

So the next sunset they stopped and foraged

hard, collecting for their waist bags a bit of everything that was not granite itself, and they kept walking as the sun's light dimmed in the eastern sky, until only a few clouds high over the eastern sea caught a dim red glow in the deep indigo; and then by the light of the million stars they stumbled on.

Even in these remote heights the trail continued to wind its way along the spine crest, weaving to north or south depending on the shape of the rock and the cliffs on each side. The trail was in poor repair and had not been used, it appeared, in years. Sometimes, because it was the only flatness in a vertical landscape, and had been crushed to sand over the centuries, it was the only foothold for the green moss, so that a mossy path extended through the white rock, a highly visible black sidewalk in the starry night. Elsewhere the trail was just a slightly less obstacle-filled track of blasted rock, and nearly impossible to see. They kept losing it and coming on it again, and each time they rediscovered it Thel felt a tiny bit of satisfaction, of communion across time with whoever had built the trail; they had both picked the same route as best. And now it was essential that they keep to that route, if they were not to come to some impassable drop-off or rise; so in places they moved on hands and knees, feeling for sand and the intangible traces of earlier feet. At times they could move their head to the side and stare straight down to the obsidian sea, flat and glossy some thousands of feet below; then they crawled, happy to hug the rock, long past talk, merely panting, gasping, from time to time whimpering or cursing under their breath, or simply groaning.

It was a long night. When dawn came and light leaked back into the world, in the hour when everything was made of translucent slabs of gray, Thel looked at the swimmer and observed that her whole shape was changing; torso longer, feet longer, ribs visible but not quite human, she was making a slow transformation back to something clearly aquatic — as she had always been, but now it was more pronounced, obvious that her race had descended from some fluid water mammal. She would be forced to crawl all the time if the transformation continued. And if her joints felt anything like his . . . he exerted the discipline, peered through the black haze of pain, saw that his own legs were thicker and his arms longer and heavier: it was a comfortable prospect to walk on all fours, and climbing the endless granite staircase of the spine was in some senses a happy challenge. Tree ancestor, he thought, and the image of a quick beautiful creature came into his mind, with the word *baboon*.

When the sun rose behind them, he looked at the ridge ahead carefully. This was the time of day when Tinou, looking back into the western dawn, would have trouble spotting them; while they looked up the ridge for him with the blaze of a nearby star as their spotlight. And eventually Thel's patience was rewarded. A head popped over the rock, just above and beyond them, a few minutes' walk only, and Tinou emerged, looked back blindly into the sun, and then hiked east up the ridge trail.

All that day they hunted him, hiding when he looked back, and so losing some ground on him. In pain as they were they could not keep pace with him in any case. But after sunset they caught sight of him, settling for the night at a flat spot in the trail.

There was still a trace of dusk in the sky when they crawled silently over the granite knobs to his camp. He was sleeping in the trail's sand, rolled in a blanket, or so they thought; but as they crept toward him his eyes opened, the whites reflecting starlight so that it seemed two glittery little jewels had popped into being, and with a laugh he said, "What persistent little things, crawling around in the night! Come out in the open, my little ones!"

He was standing over them. "My, my." Amusement made his beautiful voice bounce musically, a low fast burble. "A monkey and a water rat, it seems! Following me all this way, whatever for?" He loomed over Thel, and anger threaded into the amusement: "What kind of creature jumps through the mirror, eh? What kind of thing?"

But Thel and the swimmer were long past the snare of language, long past even much hearing Tinou's beautiful voice. He seemed to recognize this, for when they stood and approached him, spreading out to come at him from two sides, he retreated to the flat spot and his blanket.

"We want the mirror," Thel croaked, shuffling in toward him, sidling at angles in hopes of getting close more quickly than Tinou could notice. "Give it to us and we'll call it quits."

Tinou laughed and reached down into his blankets, pulled out the mirror bag. He held it out, then swung it around to throw it over the cliff into the southern sea—but he had not reckoned on Thel's new animal swiftness, and the bag crashed into Thel's upper arm as Thel rushed forward, and quicker than Thel could react or plan his numbed arm had caught Tinou by the throat and the claws of his other hand were raking Tinou's face and knocking aside the flailing arms and then with tremendous force he caught up the sorcerer's head in both hands and threw the man's whole body to the ground. The swimmer dove and bit the bent and exposed neck, and awkwardly she got to her feet and they stood watching Tinou's blood drain out of him. Mortality, how strange: that Tinou, who had given them so much, was now gone! That he had left no more behind than this! It was hard to grasp.

Thel recovered the mirror bag and checked inside it; the mirror was unbroken, its surface the color of the sky some hour or two before. Meanwhile the swimmer had taken a knife from Tinou's bag, then found a firestone and clapper. The skeleton of a dead juniper stood twisted in the lee of boulders protecting the flat, and they broke it apart right down to the ground, bashing it with rocks they could barely lift. Thel started a fire while the swimmer cut away the skin over Tinou's thighs and buttocks, and hacked out big steaks that they roasted on sticks of juniper. When they were full they slept all the way through to dawn, warmed by the coals of the fire, and their first real meal in weeks.

THIRTY

THE
GREEN FLASH

They woke in the late morning and hiked on, continuing eastward without discussion; it seemed clear to Thel that it was necessary, that they could not recross the mirror's smooth barrier on the site of Tinou's murder. That, in fact, there was a specific moment when it would be possible, a time and a place of which he knew nothing. They would have to watch. Without speaking of it he knew the swimmer had come to the same conclusion.

So they hiked on. The spine continued to rise, a granite wall splitting the sea, curving sinuously left and right, its top edge shattered over the eons into a broken split serrated knife edge of a ridge, rising unevenly as they crawled ant-like along it. Often they crawled in the literal sense, as it was too painful and precipitous to walk. The moss grew less frequently here and they were often hungry, they often recalled the delicious meal of Tinou and regretted bitterly not staying to eat all of him, or at least not taking with them his heart and liver, they drooled thinking of it. "But livers make you mad," Thel said, "someone told me. Livers and life."

Hunger made them light and they found they could almost float up smaller arêtes, just a touch here and there on the rough grainy rock, something to keep them from blowing away—to keep their shells from blowing away—everything inside having danced off on the wind. Once Thel tried to tell the swimmer how he felt about that, and he couldn't find the words to express it. He listened to the thin slow trickle of his thoughts and was surprised to hear how simple it had become: *I am climbing. I will always climb. The ocean is far below. That is a rock. I hope we find some moss.* These were his thoughts. And all that great whirling maelstrom of feeling and significance, of meaning: on the other side of the mirror, back down the peninsula among his forgotten friends, adventures, hopes, loves, dreams. All the dreams forgotten in the moment of waking, the flight that mattered so much ... it was strange to no longer desire his desires, to look at the swimmer and see a broken ancient animal, to understand that all their love had been a way of fixing time, each embrace a moment's touch of the eternal, because the caress preserves. And yet here he crawled, something like a baboon, long knuckled hairy claws at the end of furred forearms, next to something like an otter, and only her eyes remained hers, the face he remembered mostly gone, but all of it evoked by those calm black eyes unfogged by the pain that crippled her gait, clear and calm and looking around, still capable of that small ironic amused squint, as when she laid her forearm next to his and said, "Now you see why we never had children."

They had come from different worlds. They spoke different languages. What they had shared had been at least partly illusion. And yet, and yet, and yet ... He took comfort in limping along the trail beside her, before her, behind her, thumping shoulders together or sharing moss they found. Beauty is only the beginning of terror, but just to have company, to share the news: there is a block of pink quartz. The seas look high. The wind is strong. And so the terror is staved off. Through black haze, beauty still perceived.

The ridge became deeply serrated, peaks like the teeth of a crude saw, making progress nearly impossible. Why go on?, Thel thought one morning, but then the swimmer started off, scrambling up a broken cliff, using all fours, and he followed. *Why* was one of the questions that had gone away. Pain clouded his vision. A bird's nest gave them a feast. A storm left them soaked and cold. Near its end lightning shattered the peak above them, leaving their ears blasted, their nerves tingling, the strong smell of ozone in the wind. The shock of it seemed to invigorate the swimmer and she led all the next day with a will, over peak after peak, and down into deep cols. Their bodies were continuing to devolve, and only this allowed them to continue; now she could slither up rock, and how he could cling!

Then late one afternoon they made their way slowly over a hump of granite, and on the other side of it the peninsula dropped off into the sea, and came to an end.

It did so in a sheer clean prow, so smooth that it had to have been crafted. Also there was a smoothed waist-high wall to each side, bowing in and meeting at an angle, at the final point of the ridge. They walked out to the meeting of the two walls and leaned out to look. Clearly in some past age some civilization had come here and cut the granite cape smooth, creating two polished curving walls that came together in a straight edge which dropped to the sea in a single swoop, a clean crease like the bowline of a great ship. It was a drop, Thel estimated, of about ten thousand feet.

They walked around on this last forecastle, south to north and back again, looking down at the workmanship of the two cliffsides. The polished granite was a flecked color, an infinitely dense mix of feldspar, quartz, and hornblende, so that just below them it appeared speckled like a trout, while farther down it seemed only a pinkish brown, like a kind of marble. Stones that Thel dropped over the walls skipped down and disappeared, and he never even saw them mar the dark blue of the sea.

It was nearly sunset. The swimmer wandered about, collecting rocks and laying them on the triangular block where the two walls met, the outermost point. Thel asked what she was doing and she smiled, gesturing at the mirror bag. "This must be the place, yes?"

Thel shivered, looked around. They could see for many, many miles, and the horizon was a clear sharp line between sea and sky; but the air was somehow thick, the sunlight in it dark. He took the mirror from the bag and put it on the final tip of the wall, held it in place with the rocks the swimmer had gathered. The eastern sky was full of the setting sun's yellow, and the mirror's surface glowed like a lens, as if scooping up all the beautiful sunlight in the world and flinging it westward, in a single coherent beam. "But what will we do?" Thel asked.

The swimmer stretched and stood on her hind legs, pointing with one foreleg at the glass. "At the last moment of sunset we will leap through," she said happily. But she was a sea creature, and this was, perhaps, a return to the sea; while he was a tree creature, in a land without trees, and he was afraid. And yet, and yet . . .

They sat on the wall and watched the sunset, the light leaking out of the sky, the wind rustling the great space of dusk and the sea. The incredible furnace of the sun fountained light even as it sank into the ocean, which gleamed like a cut polished stone. Overhead a windhover fluttered in place, slicing the wind and sideslipping, and seeing it Thel was calmed. Whatever happened, yes, but more than that there was a kind of glory in it, to fling themselves out into the spaces they breathed, if only for one last dive or flight. The sun pared to a yellow line on the sea, and the sky darkened still; the mirror surface, still a kind of lens gathering sunlight, glowed a rich yellow that greened and greened as the sun's rays bent around the curve of the globe, prisming under gravity's pull. Out on the horizon the brilliant yellow line contracted in from both sides, greening all the while, until at last it was nothing but a single point of the most intense emerald light: the green flash, the sun's farewell, and the mirror's surface was flush with green light, the whole circle a pool of glowing green, and the swimmer's paw caught Thel by the arm and pulled him to his feet. Overhead the kestrel tipped and dove, down in a curving stoop, shooting by them and falling faster until it burst to white, like a meteor streaking over the sea; and with a cry the swimmer leaped forward and jumped through the mirror, and Thel followed fast on her heels.

About the Author

KIM STANLEY ROBINSON is the author of *The Wild Shore*, *The Gold Coast*, and *Pacific Edge*, as well as several other novels, novellas, and a nonfiction book entitled *The Novels of Philip K. Dick*. The first novel of his Martian trilogy, *Red Mars*, won the Nebula Award. *Green Mars*, the second novel of the trilogy, won the 1994 Hugo Award for Best Novel. Kim Stanley Robinson lives in Davis, California, where he is currently at work on *Blue Mars*, the third and final novel in the series.

Turn the page for a special preview of

BLUE MARS

by Kim Stanley Robinson

Kim Stanley Robinson's brilliant Martian novels have been
showered with science fiction's highest awards, and critical
and commercial acclaim. In the concluding novel of this
award-winning trilogy, the terraforming of Mars reaches its
ultimate stage. BLUE MARS is a towering completion to this
heralded saga, bringing the same level of scientific
speculation and literary power that made RED MARS and
GREEN MARS landmarks of the genre. In this early scene
from BLUE MARS, Sax faces the full fury of the new
Martian environment.
**Don't miss BLUE MARS, on sale in hardcover in
June 1996 from Bantam Spectra Books.**

Sax took a solo rover and drove it down the steep bare southern slope of Pavonis Mons, then across the saddle between Pavonis and Arsia Mons. He contoured around the great cone of Arsia Mons on its dry eastern side. After that he drove down the southern flank of Arsia, and of the Tharsis Bulge itself, until he was on the broken highlands of Daedalia Planitia. This plain was the remnant of a giant ancient impact basin, now almost entirely erased by the uptilt of Tharsis, by lava from Arsia Mons, and by the ceaseless winds, until nothing was left of the impact basin except for a collection of areologists' observations and deductions, faint radial arrays of ejecta scrapes and the like, visible on maps but not in the landscape.

To the eye as one traveled over it, it looked like much of the rest of the southern highlands: rugged bumpy pitted cracked land. A wild rockscape. The old lava flows were visible as smooth lobate curves of dark rock, like tidal swells fanning out and down. Wind streaks both light and dark marked the land, indicating dust of different weights and consistencies: there were light long triangles on the southeast sides of craters and boulders, dark chevrons to the northwest of them, and dark splotches inside the many rimless craters. The next big dust storm would redesign all these patterns.

Sax drove over the low stone waves with great pleasure, down down up, down down up, reading the sand paintings of the dust streaks like a wind chart. He was traveling not in a boulder car, with its low dark room and its cockroach scurry from one hiding place to the next, but rather in a big boxy areologist's camper, with windows on all four sides of the third-story driver's compartment. It was a very great pleasure indeed to roll along up there in the thin bright daylight, down and up, down and up, down and up over the sand-streaked plain, the horizons very distant for Mars. There was no one to hide from; no one hunting for him. He was a free man on a free planet, and if he wanted to he could drive this car right around the world. Or anywhere he pleased.

The full impact of this feeling took him about two days' drive to realize. Even then he was not sure that he comprehended it. It was a sensation of lightness, a strange lightness that caused little smiles to stretch his mouth repeatedly for no obvious reason. He had not been consciously aware, before, of any sense of oppression or fear—but it seemed it had been there—since 2061, perhaps, or the years right before it. Sixty-six years of fear, ignored and forgotten but always there—a kind of tension in the musculature, a small hidden dread at the core of things. "Sixty-six bottles of fear on the wall, sixty-six bottles of fear! Take one down, pass it around, sixty-five bottles of fear on the wall!"

Now gone. He was free, his world was free. He was driving down the wind-etched tilted plain, and earlier that day snow had begun to appear in the cracks, gleaming aquatically in a way dust never did; and then lichen; he was driving down into the atmosphere. And no reason, now, why his life ought not to continue this way, puttering about freely every day in his own world lab, and everybody else just as free as that!

It was quite a feeling.

Oh they could argue on Pavonis, and they most certainly would. Everywhere in fact. A most extraordinarily contentious lot they were. What was the sociology that would explain that? Hard to say. And in any case they had cooperated despite their bickering; it might have been only a temporary confluence of interests, but everything was temporary now—with so many traditions broken or vanished, it left what John used to call the necessity of creation; and creation was hard. Not everyone was as good at creation as they were at complaining.

But they had certain capabilities now as a group, as a—a civilization. The accumulated body of scientific knowledge was growing vast indeed, and that knowledge was giving them an array of powers that could scarcely be comprehended, even in outline, by any single individual. But powers they were, understood or not. Godlike powers, as Michel called them, though it was not necessary to exaggerate them or confuse the issue—they were powers in the material world, real but constrained by reality. Which nevertheless might allow—it looked to Sax as if they could—if rightly applied—make a decent human civilization after all. After all the many centuries of trying. And why not? Why not? Why not pitch the whole enterprise at the highest level possible? They could provide for everyone in an equitable way, they could cure disease, they could delay senescence until they lived for a thousand years, they could understand the universe from the Planck distance to the cosmic distance, from the Big Bang to the eskaton—all this was possible, it was technically achievable. And as for those who felt that humanity needed the spur of suffering to make it great, well they could go out and find anew the tragedies that Sax was sure would never go away, things like lost love, betrayal by friends, death, bad results in the lab. Meanwhile the rest of them could continue the work of making a decent civilization. They could do it! It was amazing, really. They had reached that moment in history when one could say it was possible. Very hard to believe, actually; it made Sax suspicious; in physics one became immediately dubious when a situation appeared to be somehow extraordinary or unique. The odds were against that, it suggested that it was an artifact of perspective, one had to assume that things were more or less constant and that one lived in average times—the so-called principle of mediocrity. Never a particularly attractive principle, Sax had thought; perhaps it only meant that justice had always been achievable; in any case, there it was, an extraordinary moment, right there outside his four windows, burnished under the light touch of the natural sun. Mars and its humans, free and powerful.

It was too much to grasp. It kept slipping out of his mind, then reoccurring to him, and surprised by joy he would exclaim, "Ha! Ha!" The taste of tomato soup and bread; "Ha!" The dusky purple of the twilight sky; "Ha!" The spectacle of the dashboard instrumentation, glowing faintly, reflected in the black windows;

"Ha! Ha! Ha! My-oh-my." He could drive anywhere he wanted to. No one told them what to do. He said that aloud to his darkened AI screen: "No one tells us what to do!" It was almost frightening. Vertiginous. Ka, the yonsei would say. Ka, supposedly the little red people's name for Mars, from the Japanese *ka*, meaning fire. The same word existed in several other early languages as well, including proto-Indo-European; or so the linguists said.

Carefully he got in the big bed at the back of the compartment, in the hum of the rover's heating and electrical system, and he lay humming himself under the thick coverlet that caught up his body's heat so fast, and put his head on the pillow and looked out at the stars.

The next morning a high-pressure system came in from the northwest, and the temperature rose to 262 K. He had driven down to five kilometers above the datum, and the exterior air pressure was 230 millibars. Not quite enough to breathe freely, so he pulled on one of the heated surface suits, then slipped a small air tank over his shoulders, and put its mask over his nose and mouth, and a pair of goggles over his eyes.

Even so, when he climbed out of the outer-lock door and down the steps to the sand, the intense cold caused him to sniffle and tear up, to the point of impeding his vision. The whistle of the wind was loud, though his ears were inside the hood of his suit. The suit's heater was up to the task, however, and with the rest of him warm, his face slowly got used to it.

He tightened the hood's drawstring and walked over the land. He stepped from flat stone to flat stone; here they were everywhere. He crouched often to inspect cracks, finding lichen and widely scattered specimens of other life: mosses, little tufts of sedge, grass. It was very windy. Exceptionally hard gusts slapped him four or five times a minute, with a steady gale between. This was a windy place much of the time, no doubt, with the atmosphere sliding south around the bulk of Tharsis in massed quantities. High-pressure cells would dump a lot of their moisture at the start of this rise, on the western side; indeed at this moment the horizon to the west was obscured by a flat sea of cloud, merging with the land in the far distance, out there two or three kilometers lower in elevation, and perhaps sixty kilometers away.

Underfoot there was only bits of snow, filling some of the

shaded crack systems and hollows. These snowbanks were so hard that he could jump up and down on them without leaving a mark. Windslab, partially melted and then refrozen. One scalloped slab cracked under his boots, and he found it was several centimeters thick. Under that it was powder, or granules. His fingers were cold, despite his heated gloves.

He stood again and wandered, mapless over the rock. Some of the deeper hollows contained ice pools. Around midday he descended into one of these and ate his lunch by the ice pool, lifting the air mask to take bites out of a grain-and-honey bar. Elevation 4.5 kilometers above the datum; air pressure 267 millibars. A high-pressure system indeed. The sun was low in the northern sky, a bright dot surrounded by pewter.

The ice of the pool was clear in places, like little windows giving him a view of the black bottom. Elsewhere it was bubbled or cracked, or white with rime. The bank he sat on was a curve of gravel, with patches of brown soil and black dead vegetation lying on it in a miniature berm—the high-water mark of the pond, apparently, a soil shore above the gravel one. The whole beach was no more than four meters long, one wide. The fine gravel was an umber color, piebald umber or ... He would have to consult a color chart. But not now.

The soil berm was dotted with pale green rosettes of tiny grass blades. Longer blades stood in clumps here and there. Most of the taller blades were dead, and light gray. Right next to the pond were patches of dark green succulent leaves, dark red at their edges. Where the green shaded into red was a color he couldn't name, a dark lustrous brown stuffed somehow with both its constituent colors. He would have to call up a color chart soon it seemed; lately when looking around outdoors he found that a color chart came in handy about once a minute. Waxy almost-white flowers were tucked under some of these bicolored leaves. Further on lay some tangles, red-stalked, green-needled, like beached seaweed in miniature. Again the intermixture of red and green, right there in nature staring at him.

A distant wind-washed hum; perhaps the harping rocks, perhaps the buzz of insects. Black midges, bees ... in this air they would only have to sustain about thirty millibars of CO_2, because there was so little partial pressure driving it into them, and at some point internal saturation was enough to hold any more out. For mammals that might not work so well. But they might be able to sustain twenty millibars, and with plant life flourishing all over the planet's lower elevations, CO_2 levels might drop to twenty millibars fairly soon; and then they could dispense with the air tanks and the face masks. Set loose animals on Mars.

In the faint hum of the air he seemed to hear their voices, immanent or emergent, coming in the next great surge of viriditas. The hum of distant voices; the wind; the peace of this little pool on its rocky moor; the Nirgalish pleasure he took in the sharp cold. . . . "Ann should see this," he murmured.

Then again, with the space mirrors gone, presumably everything he saw here was doomed. This was the upper limit of the biosphere, and surely with the loss of light and heat the upper limit would drop, at least temporarily, perhaps for good. He didn't like that; and it seemed possible there might be ways to compensate for the lost light. After all, the terraforming had been doing quite well before the mirrors' arrival; they hadn't been necessary. And it was good not to depend on something so fragile, and better to be rid of it now rather than later, when large animal populations might have died in the setback along with the plants.

Even so it was a shame. But the dead plant matter would only be more fertilizer in the end, and without the same kind of suffering as animals. At least so he assumed. Who knew how plants felt? When you looked closely at them, glowing in all their detailed articulation like complex crystals, they were as mysterious as any other life. And now their presence here made the entire plain, everything he could see, into one great fellfield, spreading in a slow tapestry over the rock; breaking down the weathered minerals, melding with them to make the first soils. A very slow process. There was a vast complexity in every pinch of soil; and the look of this fellfield was the loviest thing he had ever seen.

To weather. The whole world was weathering. The first printed use of the word with that meaning had appeared in a book on Stonehenge, appropriately enough, in 1665. "The weathering of so many Centuries of Years." On this stone world. Weathering. Language as the first science, exact yet vague, or multivalent. Throwing things together. The mind as weather. Or being weathered.

There were clouds coming up over the nearby hillocks to the west, their bottoms resting on a thermal layer as levelly as if pressing down on glass. Streamers like spun wool led the way east.

Sax stood up and climbed out of the pool's depression. Out of the shelter of the hole, the wind was shockingly strong—in it the cold intensified as if an ice age had struck full force that very second. Windchill factor, of course; if the temperature was 262 K, and the wind was blowing at about seventy kilometers an hour, with gusts much stronger, then the windchill factor would create a temperature equivalent of about 250 K. Was that right? That was very cold indeed to be out without a helmet. And in fact his hands were going numb. His feet as well. And his face was already without feeling, like a thick mask at the front of his head. He was shivering, and his blinks tended to stick together; his tears were freezing. He needed to get back to his car.

He plodded over the rockscape, amazed at the power of the wind to intensify cold. He had not experienced windchill like this since childhood, if then, and had forgotten how frigid one became. Staggering in the blasts, he climbed onto a low swell of the ancient lava and looked upslope. There was his rover—big, vivid green, gleaming like a spaceship—about two kilometers up the slope. A very welcome sight.

But now snow began to fly horizontally past him, giving a dramatic demonstration of the wind's great speed. Little granular pellets clicked against his goggles. He took off toward the rover, keeping his head down and watching the snow swirl over the rocks. There was so much snow in the air that he thought his goggles were fogging up, but after a painfully cold operation to wipe the insides, it became clear that the condensation was actually out in the air. Fine snow, mist, dust, it was hard to tell.

He plodded on. The next time he looked up, the air was so thick with snow that he couldn't see all the way to the rover. Nothing to do but press on. It was lucky the suit was well insulated and sewn through with heating elements, because even with the heat on at its highest power, the cold was cutting against his left side as if he were naked to the blast. Visibility extended now something like twenty meters, shifting rapidly depending on how much snow was passing by at the moment; he was in an amorphously expanding and contracting bubble of whiteness, which itself was shot through with flying snow, and what appeared to be a kind of frozen fog or mist. It seemed likely he was in the storm cloud itself. His legs were stiff. He wrapped his arms around his torso, his gloved hands trapped in his armpits. There was no obvious way of telling if he was still walking in the right direction. It seemed like he was on the same course he had been when visibility had collapsed, but it also seemed like he had gone a long way toward the rover.

There were no compasses on Mars; there were, however, APS systems in his wristpad and back in the car. He could call up a detailed map on his wristpad and then locate himself and his car on it; then walk for a while and track his positions; then make his way directly toward the car. That seemed like a great deal of work—which brought it to him that his thinking, like his body, was being affected by the cold. It wasn't that much work, after all.

So he crouched down in the lee of a boulder and tried the method. The theory behind it was obviously sound, but the instrumentation left something to be desired; the wristpad's screen was only five centimeters across, so small that he couldn't see the dots on it at all well. Finally he spotted them, walked awhile, and took another fix. But unfortunately his results indicated that he should be hiking at about a right angle to the direction he had been going.

This was unnerving to the point of paralysis. His body insisted that it had been going the right way; his mind (part of it, anyway) was pretty certain that it was better to trust the results on the wristpad, and assume that he had gotten off course somewhere. But it didn't feel that way; the ground was still at a slope that supported the feeling in his body. The contradiction was so intense that he suffered a wave of nausea, the internal torque twisting him until it actually hurt to stand, as if every cell in his body was twisting to the side against the pressure of what the wristpad was telling him—the physiological effects of a purely cognitive dissonance, it was amazing. It almost made one believe in the existence of an internal magnet in the body, as in the pineal glands of migrating birds—but there was no magnetic field to speak of. Perhaps his skin was sensitive to solar radiation to the point of being able to pinpoint the sun's location, even when the sky was a thick dark gray everywhere. It had to be something like that, because the feeling that he was properly oriented was so strong!

Eventually the nausea of the disorientation passed, and in the end he stood and took off in the direction suggested by the wristpad, feeling horrible about it, listing a little uphill just to try and make himself feel better. But one had to trust instruments over instincts, that was science. And so he plodded on, traversing the slope, shading somewhat uphill, clumsier than ever. His nearly insensible feet ran into rocks that he did not see, even though they were directly beneath him; he stumbled time after time. It was surprising how thoroughly snow could obscure the vision.

After a while he stopped, and tried again to locate the rover by APS; and his wristpad map suggested an entirely new direction, behind him and to the left.

It was possible he had walked past the car. Was it? He did not want to walk back into the wind. But now that was the way to the rover, apparently. So he ducked his head down into the biting cold and persevered. His skin was in an odd state, itching under the heating elements crisscrossing his suit, numb everywhere else. His feet were numb. It was hard to walk. There was no feeling in his face; clearly frostbite was in the offing. He needed shelter.

He had a new idea. He called up Aonia, on Pavonis, and got her almost instantly.

"Sax! Where are you?"

"That's what I'm calling about!" he said. "I'm in a storm on Daedalia! And I can't find my car! I was wondering if you would look at my APS and my rover's! And see if you can tell me which direction I should go!"

He put the wristpad right against his ear. "Ka wow, Sax." It sounded like Aonia was shouting too, bless her. Her voice was an odd addition to the scene. "Just a second, let me check! . . . Okay! There you are! And your car too! What are you doing so far south? I don't think anyone can get to you very quickly! Especially if there's a storm!"

"There is a storm," Sax said. "That's why I called."

"Okay! You're about three hundred and fifty meters to the west of your car."

"Directly west?"

"—and a little south! But how will you orient yourself?"

Sax considered it. Mars's lack of a magnetic field had never struck him as such a problem before, but there it was. He could assume the wind was directly out of the west, but that was just an assumption. "Can you check the nearest weather stations and tell me what direction the wind is coming from?" he said.

"Sure, but it won't be much good for local variations! Here, just a second, I'm getting some help here from the others."

A few long icy moments passed.

"The wind is coming from west northwest, Sax! So you need to walk with the wind at your back and a touch to your left!"

"I know. Be quiet now, until you see what course I'm making, and then correct it."

He walked again, fortunately almost downwind. After five or six painful minutes his wrist beeped.

Aonia said, "You're right on course!"

This was encouraging, and he carried on with a bit more speed, though the wind was penetrating through his ribs right to his core.

"Okay, Sax! Sax?"

"Yes!"

"You and your car are right on the same spot!"

But there was no car in view.

His heart thudded in his chest. Visibility was still some twenty meters; but no car. He had to get shelter fast. "Walk in an ever-increasing spiral from where you are," the little voice on the wrist was suggesting. A good idea in theory, but he couldn't bear to execute it; he couldn't face the wind. He stared dully at his black plastic wristpad console. No more help to be had there.

For a moment he could make out snowbanks, off to his left. He shuffled over to investigate, and found that the snow rested in the lee of a shoulder-high escarpment, a feature he did not remember seeing before, but there were some radial breaks in the rock caused by the Tharsis rise, and there must be one of them, protecting a snowbank. Snow was a tremendous insulator. Though it had little intrinsic appeal as shelter. But Sax knew mountaineers often dug into it to survive nights out. It got one out of the wind.

He stepped to the bottom of the snowbank, and kicked it with one numb foot. It felt like kicking rock. Digging a snow cave seemed out of the question. But the effort itself would warm him a bit. And it was less windy at the foot of the bank. So he kicked and kicked, and found that underneath a thick cake of windslab there was the usual powder. A snow cave might be possible after all. He dug away at it.

"Sax, Sax!" cried the voice from his wrist. "What are you doing!"

"Making a snow cave," he said. "A bivouac."

"Oh Sax—we're flying in help! We'll be able to get in

next morning no matter what, so hang on! We'll keep talking to you!"

"Fine."

He kicked and dug. On his knees he scooped out hard granular snow, tossing it into the swirling flakes flying over him. It was hard to move, hard to think. He bitterly regretted walking so far from the rover, then getting so absorbed in the landscape around that ice pond. It was a shame to get killed when things were getting so interesting. Free but dead. There was a little hollow in the snow now, through an oblong hole in the windslab. Wearily he sat down and wedged himself back into the space, lying on his side and pushing back with his boots. The snow felt solid against the back of his suit, and warmer than the ferocious wind. He welcomed the shivering in his torso, felt a vague fear when it ceased. Being too cold to shiver was a bad sign.

Very weary, very cold. He looked at his wristpad. It was four P.M. He had been walking in the storm for just over three hours. He would have to survive another fifteen or twenty hours before he could expect to be rescued. Or perhaps in the morning the storm would have abated, and the location of the rover become obvious. One way or another he had to survive the night by huddling in a snow cave. Or else venture out again and find the rover. Surely it couldn't be far away. But until the wind lessened, he could not bear to be out looking for it.

He had to wait in the snow cave. Theoretically he could survive a night out, though at the moment he was so cold it was hard to believe that. Night temperatures on Mars still plummeted drastically. Perhaps the storm might lessen in the next hour, so that he could find the rover and get to it before dark.

He told Aonia and the others where he was. They sounded very concerned, but there was nothing they could do. He felt irritation at their voices.

It seemed many minutes before he had another thought. When one was chilled, blood flow was greatly reduced to the limbs—perhaps that was true for the cortex as well, the blood going preferentially to the cerebellum where the necessary work would continue right to the end.

More time passed. Near dark, it appeared. Should call out again. He was *too* cold—something seemed wrong. Advanced age, altitude, CO_2 levels—some factor or combination of factors was making it worse than it should be. He could die of exposure in a single night. Appeared in fact to be doing just that. Such a storm! Loss of the mirrors, perhaps. Instant ice age. Extinction event.

The wind was making odd noises, like shouts. Powerful gusts no doubt. Like faint shouts, howling "Sax! Sax! Sax!"

Had they flown someone in? He peered out into the dark storm, the snowflakes somehow catching the late light and tearing overhead like dim white static.

Then between his ice-crusted eyelashes he saw a figure emerge out of the darkness. Short, round, helmeted. "Sax!" The sound was distorted, it was coming from a loudspeaker in the figure's helmet. Those Da Vinci techs were very resourceful people. Sax tried to respond, and found he was too cold to speak. Just moving his boots out of the hole was a stupendous effort. But it appeared to catch this figure's eye, because it turned and strode purposefully through the wind, moving like a skillful sailor on a bouncing deck, weaving this way and that through the slaps of the gusts. The figure reached him and bent down and grabbed Sax by the wrist, and he saw its face through the faceplate, as clear as through a window. It was Hiroko.

She smiled her brief smile and hauled him up out of his cave, pulling so hard on his left wrist that his bones creaked painfully.

"Ow!" he said.

Out in the wind the cold was like death itself. Hiroko pulled his left arm over her shoulder, and, still holding hard to his wrist just above the wristpad, she led him past the low escarpment and right into the teeth of the gale.

"My rover is near," he mumbled, leaning hard on her and trying to move his legs fast enough to make steady plants of the foot. So good to see her again. A solid little person, very powerful as always.

"It's over here," she said through her loudspeaker. "You were pretty close."

"How did you find me?"

"We were tracking you as you came down Arsia. Then today when the storm hit I checked you out, and saw you were out of your rover. After that I came out to see how you were doing."

"Thanks."

"You have to be careful in storms."

Then they were standing before his rover. She let go of his

wrist, and it throbbed painfully. She bonked her faceplate against his goggles. "Go on in," she said.

He climbed carefully up the steps to the rover's lock door; opened it; fell inside. He turned clumsily to make room for Hiroko, but she wasn't in the door. He leaned back out into the wind, looked around. No sight of her. It was dusk; the snow now looked black. "Hiroko!" he cried.

No answer.

He closed the lock door, suddenly frightened. Oxygen deprivation—He pumped the lock, fell through the inside door into the little changing room. It was shockingly warm, the air a steamy blast. He plucked ineffectively at his clothes, made no progress. He went at it more methodically. Goggles and face mask off. They were coated with ice. Ah—possibly his air supply had been restricted by ice in the tube between tank and mask. He sucked in several deep breaths, then sat still through another bout of nausea. Pulled off his hood, unzipped the suit. It was almost more than he could do to get his boots off. Then the suit. His underclothes were cold and clammy. His hands were burning as if on fire. It was a good sign, proof that he was not substantially frostbitten; nevertheless it was agony.

His whole skin began to buzz with the same inflamed pain. What caused that, return of blood to capillaries? Return of sensation to chilled nerves? Whatever it was, it hurt almost unbearably. "Ow!"

He was in excellent spirits. It was not just that he had been spared from death, which was nice; but that Hiroko was alive. Hiroko was alive! It was incredibly good news. Many of his friends had assumed all along that she and her group had slipped away from the assault on Sabishii, moving through that town's mound maze back out into their system of hidden refuges; but Sax had never been sure. There was no evidence to support the idea. And there were elements in the security forces perfectly capable of murdering a group of dissidents and disposing of their bodies. This, Sax had thought, was probably what had happened. But he had kept this opinion to himself, and reserved judgment. There had been no way of knowing for sure.

But now he knew. He had stumbled into Hiroko's path, and she had rescued him from death by freezing, or asphyxiation, whichever came first. The sight of her cheery, somehow impersonal face—her brown eyes—the feel of her body supporting him—her hand clamped over his wrist . . . he would have a bruise because of that. Perhaps even a sprain. He flexed his hand, and the pain in his wrist brought tears to his eyes, it made him laugh. Hiroko!

After a time the fiery return of sensation to his skin banked down. Though his hands felt bloated and raw, and he did not have proper control of his muscles, or his thoughts, he was basically getting back to normal. Or something like normal.

"Sax! Sax! Where are you? Answer us, Sax!"

"Ah. Hello there. I'm back in my car."

"You found it? You left your snow cave?"

"Yes. I—I saw my car, in the distance, through a break in the snow."

They were happy to hear it.

He sat there, barely listening to them babble, wondering why he had spontaneously lied. Somehow he was not comfortable telling them about Hiroko. He assumed that she would want to stay concealed; perhaps that was it. Covering for her. . . .

He assured his associates that he was all right, and got off the phone. He pulled a chair into the kitchen and sat on it. Warmed soup and drank it in loud slurps, scalding his tongue. Frostbitten, scalded, shaky—slightly nauseous—once weeping—mostly stunned—despite all this, he was very, very happy. Sobered by the close call, of course, and embarrassed or even ashamed at his ineptitude, staying out, getting lost and so on—all very sobering indeed—and yet still he was happy. He had survived, and even better, so had Hiroko. Meaning no doubt that all of her group had survived with her, including the half dozen of the First Hundred who had been with her from the beginning, Iwao, Gene, Rya, Raul, Ellen, Evgenia. . . . Sax ran a bath and sat in the warm water, adding hotter water slowly as his body core warmed; and he kept returning to that wonderful realization. A miracle—well not a miracle of course—but it had that quality, of unexpected and undeserved joy.

When he found himself falling asleep in the bath he got out, dried off, limped on sensitive feet to his bed, crawled under the coverlet, and fell asleep, thinking of Hiroko. Of making love with her in the baths in Zygote, in the warm relaxed lubriciousness of their bathhouse trysts, late at night when everyone else was asleep. Of her hand clamped on his wrist, pulling him up. His left wrist was very sore. And that made him happy.

Bantam Spectra publishes more Hugo and Nebula Award-winning
novels than any other science fiction and fantasy imprint..
Celebrate Spectra—read them all!

HUGO WINNERS

A CANTICLE FOR LEIBOWITZ, Walter M. Miller, Jr.	_____27381-7 $5.99/$6.99
THE GODS THEMSELVES, Isaac Asimov	_____28810-5 $5.99/$6.99
RENDEZVOUS WITH RAMA, Arthur C. Clarke	_____28789-3 $6.50/$8.99
DREAMSNAKE, Vonda N. McIntyre	_____29659-0 $5.99/$7.50
FOUNDATION'S EDGE, Isaac Asimov	_____29338-9 $5.99/$6.99
STARTIDE RISING, David Brin	_____27418-X $5.99/$6.99
THE UPLIFT WAR, David Brin	_____27971-8 $5.99/$6.99
HYPERION, Dan Simmons	_____28368-5 $5.99/$6.99
DOOMSDAY BOOK, Connie Willis	_____56273-8 $5.99/$6.99
GREEN MARS, Kim Stanley Robinson	_____37335-8 $12.95/$16.95

NEBULA WINNERS

THE GODS THEMSELVES, Isaac Asimov	_____28810-5 $5.99/$6.99
RENDEZVOUS WITH RAMA, Arthur C. Clarke	_____28789-3 $6.50/$8.99
DREAMSNAKE, Vonda N. McIntyre	_____29659-0 $5.99/$7.50
THE FOUNTAINS OF PARADISE, Arthur C. Clarke	_____28819-9 $5.99/$6.99
TIMESCAPE, Gregory Benford	_____27709-0 $5.99/$6.99
STARTIDE RISING, David Brin	_____27418-X $5.99/$6.99
TEHANU, Ursula K. Le Guin	_____28873-3 $6.50/$7.99
DOOMSDAY BOOK, Connie Willis	_____56273-8 $5.99/$6.99
RED MARS, Kim Stanley Robinson	_____56073-5 $5.99/$7.50